LADY IN RED

One night, two senseless murders... DI Lorraine Hunt and her team are no strangers to serious cases – but the evidence seems to point to someone very close at hand... In this, the sixth of her Seahills crime novels, Sheila Quigley brings us back to the close-knit community in Houghton le Spring, County Durham. Her fans worldwide will not be disappointed...

LADY IN RED

LADY IN RED

by

Sheila Quigley

Magna Large Print Books
Long Preston, North Yorkshire,
BD23 4ND, England.

British Library Cataloguing in Publication Data.

Quigley, Sheila
Lady in red.

A catalogue record of this book is available from the British Library

ISBN 978-0-7505-4047-6

First published in Great Britain in 2014 by Burgess Books

Cover illustration © Ilona Wellman by arrangement with Arcangel Images

The moral right of the author has been asserted

Published in Large Print 2015 by arrangement with
Sheila Quigley

Magna Large Print is an imprint of Library Magna Books Ltd.

Printed and bound in Great Britain by
T.J. (International) Ltd., Cornwall, PL28 8RW

PROLOGUE

'OK, spread them.'

'You fucking kidding, or what?'

'Just thought I'd save us all a bit of time.' The guard, a dead ringer for Morgan Freeman, grinned at him.

'I'm on me way out, you prick,' the man snarled at the guard. He was dark haired and blue eyed, sporting four days of stubble, wearing a grey hoodie with a cream baseball cap.

'Yeah, so you say, but we all know you'll soon be back. Your sort always are.'

'Fuck off with the lecture.'

The gates opened, the man stubbornly not complying with the guard's wishes. The now ex-prisoner, hoodie up over his baseball cap so that only the peak was on show, shadowing most of his face, clenched his fists at the slowness of them. He could taste freedom on his skin. Even the air smelled different. He took the first step.

One more he thought, just one more, and I'm on my way.

Taking a deep breath, he took the next step. He was free. Free to do whatever he wanted to do.

Turning, he stuck his middle finger up at the guard. The guard, used to the ways of those who never learn, shook his head as he pressed the button to close the gates, and watched as the man did what most newly released prisoners did.

For a moment, the young man stood staring up at the walls that had held him prisoner for more than three years. With a sneer, and yet another snarl for the guard, who just stared blank faced at him, he turned and walked away.

'Fuck off, twat,' he muttered under his breath.

Yes, I probably will be back, but it'll be worth it. After all, it's the only home I've ever had, he thought, heading towards the centre of Durham. He looked around as he walked. Nothing much had changed in Durham since he'd been banged up, lots of students hanging around, mixing with tourists as usual.

Nice to have a chance at life. Bastards.

He reached the market place, where a statue of a man on a horse dominated the square. He looked up at the statue, the third Marquess of Londonderry, then swung his eyes to the second statue, Neptune. What the fuck is a sea king doing in the middle of Durham, for fuck's sake? Stupid.

He'd had plenty of time to read up about Durham and the neighbouring towns, which were far from where he'd been dumped as a baby all those years ago. He knew that Neptune was there because of a plan in 1720 to change the course of the River Wear to turn Durham into a seaport, which didn't happen. He also knew just about everything there was to know about the neighbouring towns – well, everything he needed to know about one in particular.

Walking past the church on the corner, he passed the ancient indoor market and went on up to WH Smiths, where he bought a newspaper and a bar of chocolate. Smiling at the pretty young blonde behind the counter, he said, 'Fancy a good time?' He looked her slowly up and down, stripping her with his eyes.

Ignoring him, but unable to control the involuntary shiver that coursed through her body, the girl put his change on the counter rather than into his hand, and turned to the next customer.

'OK, your loss.' He muttered, as shrugging he left the shop and sat on one of the benches in the market place. He watched as a Tour guide filled in a bunch of Norwegian tourists about the rich heritage of Durham city. With another sneer in their direction, he opened his newspaper and hid himself from all the hustle going on around him. It would take a while. The crowds would be a problem at first, but he'd soon get used to it.

It wasn't the first time he'd been banged up for violence, then let out to do it again.

A few minutes later, a teenage girl in a black hoodie and skinny jeans, on a bright yellow skateboard, just missed knocking into him. The urge to grab the kid and knock seven kinds of shit out of her was strong. But the man resisted. He had work to do.

Work that nothing could distract him from.

Work that had been waiting for over twenty-three years.

Work that had been in the planning stage before he even entered the infants' school.

And now the time had come, thanks to the internet and his recently released cellmate, and hadn't that been fate! He now had all the information he'd craved for years, every tiny detail. Folding his newspaper and dropping the wrapper from his chocolate bar onto the ground between his feet, he rose, took one more look around, and headed for the bus station.

He passed a plump, dark haired woman who, smiling and in broken English, tried to sell him a copy of the *Big Issue*. He looked into her eyes, and the woman froze for a moment. Stepping quickly back, she knocked her chair over, and her bag containing most of her copies fell to the floor, spilling over the pavement. The man looked at them with contempt, gave another withering glance at the woman, then walked away.

Reaching the bus station, he looked up the times for the bus he wanted.

'Five minutes,' he muttered.

He almost laughed out loud. Five minutes, five whole minutes. It was nothing, nothing at all, a tiny glitch in time not to be compared with the years he'd waited.

Walking over to his stop, he fell into the queue behind an old couple who were babbling on about the cathedral. Ignoring them wasn't easy, as both of them appeared to be deaf from the way they were shouting. He concentrated on the task in hand, until the bus arrived for Houghton le Spring.

DAY ONE

CHAPTER ONE

Karen MacDonald, her blonde ponytail bobbing from side to side as she finished dressing the two mannequins in her shop window in red silk negligees, stepped back to admire her handiwork. She was unaware that she was being watched from across the road by a very tall Santa with an extra long white beard, who had been standing there shaking his charity tin for most of the day. Although to Karen, everybody was tall. Barely reaching five foot, she had to look up to just about everyone.

Karen had moved to Houghton le Spring from Galashiels six months ago, following her truck driver boyfriend (much to his surprise) to his hometown, and opened the shop five weeks later. He had not been too happy about the move, and strongly insisted that she take a flat in Durham, definitely not Houghton le Spring. She was never ever to mention his name to anyone who came into the shop, in case his boys found out. He thought it would be much better coming from him that he had a girlfriend, and he wanted to find the right time to tell them himself.

Always eager to please, Karen had gone along with his plans, happy that he visited her at least twice a week. Well, sometimes. Sometimes it would be a week or two before she saw him. She paused for a moment, staring into space, and her heart dropped. A couple of times, but that had been the first week, now it was more like once every two weeks, she sighed, and fussed around the mannequins.

She knew he was very busy with his lorry driving job, which kept him on the road and away from home for most of the week, and the two handicapped children he had took up a lot of his time. He had told her that he and the boys lived with his widowed mother, since his wife died in a tragic accident over five years ago. His mother took care of the boys while he was on the road.

But tomorrow, finally, after much begging on her part, she was at last going to meet his family. She could feel the excitement building up inside of her. She couldn't understand why it had taken so long, but she hadn't liked to pressure him too much as sometimes he got quite angry. The last thing she wanted to do was lose him. She'd lost so much already.

Remembering her family in Scotland, and feeling sad again, she looked out the window, noticing that Santa had finally gone and the street was mostly empty. At least a third of the shops were shuttered. Large white snowflakes spiralled slowly from the dark sky. As yet there was no covering, but Karen suspected that there soon would be.

'Well, Sheba.' She smiled at her white Persian cat, who had travelled from Galashiels with her, and now sat happily cleaning her paws on a pink satin cushion near the window. 'It's the season for red, all right.'

She thought of the new red dress hanging in her wardrobe and sighed. He'd freaked out when she'd shown it to him, and forbidden her to ever wear it. For a moment she'd been quite frightened, as she'd watched his hands clench into fists. Her backward steps into the kitchen table, resulting in the dinner being spilt off the plates, had made him even more angry. He'd stormed out that night, and she'd been terrified he was never coming back.

But she had just been silly, stupid silly. Of course she had, he would never hit her. He's the kindest man I've ever met, and he's always right, with only my best interests at heart, nodding, she convinced herself yet again, remembering him saying over and over how much he loved her, and that he only wanted to protect her. That's why she could only shop in the corner shop next to her flat, and why she was to come straight to work on a morning and straight home on a night.

There are many evil people out there, he kept telling her.

She nodded again to herself. He's right, of course. After all, he really does love me.

Slowly she ran a piece of red tinsel through her fingers, admiring the way it glittered in the spotlights.

'Wonder what he buys me for Christmas, Sheba?' She wrapped the tinsel around her engagement finger in hope, and held it up to the light, picturing a beautiful ruby engagement ring, her heartbeat rising at the thought.

The cat ignored her, as cats do. Sheba was too busy watching something out the corner of her eye.

Karen started to sing, halfway through the chorus of her favourite karaoke song, *Lady in Red*. It had been a long time since she'd been to a karaoke, and she was forbidden to sing in front of him. He didn't like women singing.

She stopped singing and chewed her lip. She'd puzzled for a while now about why he'd not been at all happy when he'd found out about her move here. But what else was she supposed to do? She'd fallen out with her family, who did not like him one bit. As far as her sister Rose was concerned, it had been hate at first sight, for both parties. Her brother James had called him a wanker, and refused to speak to her while she was with him. Rose had actually thrown a cup of water in her face, and told her to wake up and realise she was in love with a control freak.

They just didn't understand, any of them. Then her parents had demanded that she see sense and choose.

It had been hard, but they refused to realise just how she felt. Yes, he was worth giving up her singing career for. To be honest, it wasn't going anywhere. And he was right – she was a bit bored with her horse, and there just wasn't enough time to look after Flame properly since she'd met him. Although selling Flame had not been easy.

She sighed. Flame had been the most loving of horses, and she prayed that the home he'd gone to was kind to him. For a moment, the thought of her pet brought a tear to her eye.

What hurt the most, though, was that her boyfriend had not even visited her shop once. Everything that had to be done she'd done herself, painting all the walls a deep cream and paying for shelves and extra electric points, because he'd been too busy with extra work loads – even a trip to Europe for three weeks, delivering furniture to half a dozen little countries.

She shook her head, as her instinct to defend the man she adored took over and her doubts started to melt.

Really, he is so busy. His poor boys take up so much of his time when he's home, he's such a brilliant father. If I'm going to be a mother to his kids, I must learn to share him.

Then all doubt was gone, again.

Happily she looked at the tinsel round her finger and muttered. 'The reason he hasn't been to see the shop is because he's so busy, that's why. Course he is. He will come.' She nodded, her blue eyes shining and a satisfied smile on her face.

She never saw the hackles start to rise on the back of the cat's neck, nor her lips pull back from her sharp teeth in a silent hiss, as Karen removed the glittery engagement ring.

A second later, Karen's smile changed to a grimace. Her eyes widened in fear as a hand grabbed her face from behind, and the heels of her feet beat out a drum roll as she was dragged away from the shop window.

CHAPTER TWO

Detective Sergeant Luke Daniels lifted his glass to his mouth and swallowed the last of his drink. With exaggerated carefulness he managed to put the empty glass on the bar, then looked towards the double doors of the pub, wishing that they would both keep still. Tall, well built, black, wearing jeans and a pale blue shirt, Luke tried to judge the distance from the bar to the revolving doors. He was sure they were ordinary doors when he came in.

Weren't they?

Course they were!

He shook his head, which only made things worse. Since when did the Beehive have revolving doors? He looked at the doors again, frowning.

Definitely revolving.

'Have another, Luke. Come on, mate, just one more. Go for it. In a few days' time I'll have the ball and chain on, won't I, and things ain't ever gonna be the same again.' Detective Matt Abrahams, balding before his time and as tall as Luke, was one of Luke's old school friends who worked out of Newcastle. He was celebrating his stag party, and slurred his words as he rocked from side to side.

Luke rocked with him, the motion making him feel sick. 'Whoa... Gotta go.' He raised his hand to pat Matt's shoulder, missed, and nearly toppled over. He was saved from falling flat on his face by Jacko Musgrove who was passing. He grabbed Luke's shoulders and helped him straighten up.

'Think you've had more than enough, mate,' Jacko grinned, straightening his eye patch, which Luke had knocked askew with his elbow. He squeezed past the other four members of the stag party and parked himself at the far side of the bar, where he was finishing his own drink off. His friends, cousins Danny and Len Jordan, had already left, and he was busy thinking over Danny's latest crazy idea of how to make cash. He shook his head. Danny was a crackerjack. His new plan was edging more and more into not only illegal, but downright fantasy.

Luke shook his head, another mistake, as he slowly muttered a delayed 'Thank you', which Jacko acknowledged with a smile.

Luke frowned to himself, as he heaved a big sigh and wondered why he felt so over the top. He wasn't a big drinker by any means. But four pints of lager?

Was it four?

Or only three?

Might have been five... Five, tops.

No way, not that many!

Whatever, I shouldn't really feel as drunk as this.

God, I think I'm dying!

He squinted up at the clock, then slowly looked around the bar. 'Where's those kids gone?' he muttered.

Three strangers had come in earlier and stood next to Luke. One of them kept grinning like an idiot, repeatedly demanding whiskey, which the landlord refused to serve him. After a five minute argument in which they insisted they were over eighteen, and forgotten their ID, the one who was the mouthpiece of the group squeezed past Luke in his attempt to reach the bar. The other two moved even closer until they were stopped by Luke, who had visions of them climbing over him in their attempt to get to the bar, because they were so close. They had finally settled for cans of Coke, after they had mouthed off about there only being Diet Coke left.

He shrugged. Actually, he might have seen a couple of them around, but couldn't put a name to the faces. They've probably crawled into some dive, he thought, then muttered as his stomach settled, 'What the hell... I'll just have one more. Coming home soon, Lorry. Love you, Lorry.'

'Yeah, right,' Matt grinned.

'Cannot believe you're marrying my baby sister, Matt.' Detective James Dinwall said, as Luke hesitantly raised a very shaky finger to the landlord.

Ducking out of Luke's way before he lost an eye, Matt grinned at Dinwall. 'Better than marrying you, and that's a fact. And I thought you would have got rid of the pony-tail, unless you secretly want to be a brides-maid.' He slapped Dinwall's arm. 'Yes, that's it isn't it?' Laughing loudly, he went on, 'Shame pink's not your colour.'

Dinwall, in his late thirties, had worn his long dark hair in a ponytail for as long as anyone could remember. Medium height and stocky, he always liked to have the last word.

'He'll look better in lemon, don't you think?' Carter put in, quite bravely for him.

Dinwall glared at him. 'Better than you will, Ginge, and that's a fine fact.'

Carter blushed between his freckles.

Satisfied to be one up, Dinwall then turned to Matt and said, 'Well, I had a think about the hair. Even asked the fan club. They – and me – said, "No way."'

'Fan-club? You being the one and only member, of course?' Matt snorted.

'Something like that.' Dinwall grinned, then nodding wisely went on. 'Actually people that's for me to know and you lot to wonder.'

'Gotta ... gotta ... go. Really gotta go,' Luke said, slurring his words. All thoughts of another drink left his head as everyone, including the landlord, laughed.

'What's the matter? You can't keep up with the rest of us? Dinwall winked at Matt.

Luke slowly shook his head, which was a big mistake, a very big mistake. Vast waves of dizziness threatened to send him crashing to the floor. 'What the hell?' he mumbled.

'Fucking hell. Even Carter can drink more than you can,' Dinwall said, just managing to bite his tongue and stop himself from calling Luke a pussy. Blushing even more,

Carter swung his adoring eyes from Luke and fixed them firmly on the wall above Dinwall's head, and muttered. 'Sure, yes... Let's all have one more for the road.'

'Yeah.' Travis looked at the clock. 'It's gone eleven. Guess I better be making tracks home. But before we split – how about a toast to Peters?'

Everyone nodded. Peters had been shot dead by a crazed gunman four months previously in the house their boss had shared with her mother Mavis and God-mother Peggy. As they all raised their glasses and said, 'To Peters', Luke gagged and quickly made his way to the toilets.

CHAPTER THREE

Detective Inspector Lorraine Hunt of Houghton le Spring CID yawned as she pulled her pink fluffy dressing gown on over her winceyette passion-killer pink pyjamas. The dressing gown and pyjamas were last year's unwanted Christmas present from her godmother Peggy, aka The Rock Chick. She wouldn't ever dream of buying them for herself. Maybes for her mother. Just maybes, though. She had looked at them with the dismay with which she looked at most presents from Peggy, and thought she would never wear them for at least fifty years.

Peggy was a past master at buying unwanted gifts. 'But... I guess this time they've come in handy.'

She had dug them out of the bottom drawer, only remembering them because she'd just thrown them in there a few hours ago. They were still wrapped in the cellophane bag they'd come in. It was damn cold tonight and, seeing as it was only her second night living here, she wasn't sure – actually she didn't have a clue – where the heating panel was. Certainly it wasn't in the most obvious places. She hadn't wanted to phone Luke and ask, in case he and the other guys thought she was keeping tabs on him already. She channel-hopped again, sighed and threw the remote down beside her. 'Nowt but flaming repeats and stupid cookery programmes. For God's sake, the whole world should be able to cook by now, there's so flaming many of them!' Sighing, she pulled the hair band and clips out of her blonde hair, letting it fall free around her shoulders.

She glanced at the clock, agitated because Luke had promised he would be in pretty early. She had cooked his favourite, gammon steak with all the trimmings, which was now looking like a soggy mess, and belonged nowhere else but in the bin after three hours keeping warm in the oven.

'House-trained I'm fucking not, mate. That'll be the first and the last you get,' she muttered.

She glared with narrowed eyes at the large clock on the wall above the fire. 'Half past fucking eleven? Jesus, where the hell are you, Luke?'

A moment later, she jumped slightly when a red bauble suddenly, and for no apparent reason, fell off the silver Christmas tree in the window. She watched it roll under the table that the tree stood on, remembering their first argument. After carting her belongs in last night, they had decided to dress the Christmas tree. She had suggested a quick trip to the shops, some new shiny baubles – she thought gold would look good. But Luke didn't like gold on silver, and had argued that the red ones he already had, which used to belong to his mother, were still perfectly all right. Red was his favourite colour.

They might have been all right, if they weren't battered and broken when he opened the box to show her. The amazement on his face had made her laugh. A quick visit to Tesco's had produced a fine couple of boxes of mixed red and gold shiny baubles. With Selina, Luke's teenage daughter, giving her approval via phone, Luke had to grin and bear it.

She sighed. She did love him, although

there had been no more mention of marriage since that awful night when they had all been at the mercy of a crazed gunman. She kept wondering if he'd got cold feet.

Well, I'm not gonna bring it up.

So, if he doesn't want to marry me, why did he ask me to move in?

And where the fucking hell are you?

She sighed. Perhaps she was being a bit harsh. It was, after all, the stag night for one of his best friends.

'OK, I am being a bit harsh,' she muttered. 'But it's friggin' freezing in here.'

Picking up her mobile, she frowned as she checked for messages. 'Damn.' She threw the mobile down on the couch next to the remote, and made her way towards the stairs. She turned back, suddenly remembering the broken bauble, knowing she wouldn't be able to sleep until she found out why it had fallen off the tree. Bending down, she rummaged under the table. After a moment, she found it. Examining it closely, she saw that it was one of the new ones, the string attached to the top having snapped for no apparent reason.

'Hope they're all not going to drop to bits,' she muttered, scowling at the baubles as she climbed to her feet.

'Guess Luke's right, they make nowt to last these days.' Putting the bauble on the table, she went into the hallway. Checking that the door was locked, she then headed up the stairs to bed. 'You just better have your key, mister. And you dare wake me up when you finally do crawl home!'

Halfway up, she changed her mind and decided to give him one more call. In the last twenty-four hours since she'd finally fully committed and moved in with Luke (and his daughter Selina, who was spending the week in Blackpool with her boyfriend Mickey), he'd never once been late. 'Well, I guess twenty-four hours are nothing to go by.' She shrugged. But in fact, Luke was never late for anything. He was the most dependable man she had ever met in her life.

Definitely more dependable than her ex, and that was a fact. With a sigh, she headed quickly back downstairs, and rummaged under the cushion on the new cream leather settee they had chosen together, for her mobile, only to find out a moment later that his was still switched off.

'For fuck's sake!' She stormed back up the stairs.

'Ow!' she yelled, a few moments later, when she stubbed her toe on the top stair. 'Your fault, Luke,' she muttered, massaging her toe.

Five minutes later as she lay on her bed staring up at the ceiling, she wondered why she'd felt so angry. Really, she shouldn't have. Luke was one of the best men she'd ever known. She put it down to the lousy day she'd had. Usually her judgement was spot on, but she'd had a man accused of rape hung drawn and quartered, even though he'd been adamant that he was innocent. He'd screamed at the top of his lungs, as he was dragged to his cell, that the woman was a nutter and he'd wanted nothing to do with her for months, that it was her who was stalking him, not the other way round. She'd actually laughed in the face of this six foot, broad shouldered man, as the girl, under five foot and very petite, had painted a good picture of a very bullying brute.

Until a little digging on Sanderson's part had found out that the girl had already accused two other men of raping her, one in Birmingham and the other in Newcastle. Both cases had gone to trial and been found innocent.

What the hell gets into some women that they crave attention so much that they would go down that route? Same as those with that hospital syndrome, I suppose, who harm themselves or their kids on purpose, just for the attention that they crave.

She sighed, more angry at herself than Luke, because she'd let her vision become clouded. She turned on her side. A moment later she was back up, stripping off the winceyette pyjamas, finding them far too restricting. Lying back down, she snuggled into her quilt. Her eyelids started to flutter, and a few moments later she was fast asleep.

CHAPTER FOUR

Luke threw up, and then dipped his head under the coldwater tap to revive himself. It didn't do much good. In fact, he was starting to feel even worse. He walked back into the bar just as the door closed behind his friends. He looked around. The only person left in the Beehive was the landlord, Jimmy Foley, who looked at him with a frown, then pointedly turned to the clock and then back to Luke, with a raised eyebrow. Luke got the hint and, with a sigh and a lift of his hand, headed out the door with Foley, key in hand, right behind him.

After staggering across the car park, bouncing off a car and apologising, and falling down twice, he set off for home still swaying from side to side, knowing he would well and truly be in the doghouse.

'We should get a dog,' he muttered.

With the next breath, he shook his head. 'No. My Lorraine already has Duke. Lovely dog... Lovely dog, Duke...'

He giggled. 'I so love dogs.' Then he

patted the air at his side as if he was patting a dog's head. 'Good Duke. Good boy.'

He continued walking in a sort of two steps forward, one back kind of way, and muttering to himself, even once or twice breaking into song. He was a staunch Bee Gees fan, and loved the song, *Tragedy*. For a further ten minutes he tortured the night with his singing, until suddenly he stopped.

'What the...?'

He stared around in amazement. 'What the flaming hell am I doing here?'

He had no recollection at all of walking up to the town centre, the opposite direction to home, nor had he seen the shadows flickering amongst the buildings behind him. He did, though, feel the pavement hit his face, as he was jumped on from behind and brought down with a heavy crash.

DAY TWO

CHAPTER FIVE

There was a fierce wind blowing, and the dry, powdery snowfall from last night was being moved around Houghton le Spring's main street in short sharp gusts.

'Bloody hell! That's a bit close to the bone.' Sandra Gilbride said, staring into the shop window as she pushed her auburn hair away from her face. Usually Sandra, lover of the highest heels imaginable, wore her long hair in a single plait which hung down her back, but this morning there had been no time, as Doris had been knocking on her door before eight o'clock. Even the offer of a cuppa hadn't tempted her to wait for the next bus.

'What is?' Doris Musgrove asked.

The pair had just stepped off the early bus, hoping to get some last minute shopping done before the street filled up with Christmas shoppers, scouring the shops as if there would soon be nothing left. Sandra had her Christmas box money from her husband, with instructions that she had to buy the red dress she liked in M & Co's window. He really has such a thing about red, she thought with a smile. If he had his way, everything I wear from me knickers to me coat would be red.

She glanced down at her red coat and shrugged. Another present from him. She frowned as her thoughts wandered. Things had been really tight these last few years, helping the boys out at university, with two more boys to go, and the mortgage increasing yearly. Sandra's was one of only a few bought houses on the Seahills, and she'd always been proud of the fact. Yet, she wondered, even though money was tight, he still kept buying her clothes. Red clothes, especially. Lately, some of the stuff had been quite kinky.

She sighed. He's probably suffering some sort of midlife crisis. She focused back on the window display.

Doris had a purse full of money from her son Jacko to buy presents with. Playing the lottery had at long last paid off. Jacko had won seven hundred pounds last week, and God bless him, the bulk had gone to Doris for Christmas shopping. For the first year in as long as she could remember, she wouldn't be struggling to pay a loan off to them greedy filthy horrible sharks. It had taken until this September to pay the last one off, when Jacko had found out and gone calling with a few friends, and got the extortionate interest knocked off. And hadn't that eased her breathing!

She'd already seen a nice dark brown coat

she fancied. Only Jacko had said if she came back with anything brown he would burn it, as she was starting to look more and more like a clone of her best friend Dolly Smith everyday. She tufted as she leaned forward. So what if she liked to wear brown? It was her choice. Dolly didn't have the monopoly on it.

'That man– Look! Look at that dummy! It's got no friggin' clothes on.' Sandra said suddenly, and very loudly.

Doris pulled a face as she peered through the window. She stared at the naked dummy, sitting on a chair between two others wearing red negligees. She tutted. 'First time you've seen a store dummy with no clothes on, like?' She peered again at the mannequin, noticed its right hand was missing, although it was wearing a see-through red glove. Then she looked at the other two mannequins. Both had missing pieces. In the corner of the window was an assortment of limbs, plus two heads facing away from them, one brunette one blonde.

'First time I've ever seen one with pubes, and that's a fact. Especially as real looking as those.'

'What the hell's pubes?' Doris asked, leaning in closer to the window and peering at the other mannequin. Sandra shot her a look of total disbelief.

A moment later, Sandra shrugged and,

unable to contain a smile – in fact, she was biting her lip to stop herself laughing out loud – thought, well, I suppose you kind of forget Doris is over seventy. Probably didn't even call them that back in her day.

The smile quickly fell from her face, and she screamed as a white cat with blood red paws jumped onto the mannequin, then to the windowsill, and ran along it leaving bloody paw prints in its wake. She screamed again a moment later as, disturbed by the cat, the mannequin toppled over to reveal a knife sticking out of its back.

'Jesus!' Doris yelled, as the cat started pawing at the window an inch from her face, leaving streaks of red on the glass. Pulling herself upright, she nearly succeeded in knocking Sandra onto the road. She practically jumped out of her skin when a passing blue van pipped at her.

'It's real ... oh, my God, Sandra.' Doris, her eyes wide and her mouth open in shock, turned to Sandra. 'It ... it's that new shop-keeper. I didn't realise at first, cos ... because her hair was all over her face, thought it was just another dummy, but it's her I know it is. Poor bugger hasn't been here five minutes, she ... she belongs in Scotland... And look ... look.' She pointed at the cat's paws. 'Oh, my God! Look, it's all over his back end and underneath, Jesus, he must have been rolling in the blood... Oh, the poor, poor thing.'

Sandra was rubbing her chin with her left hand where the top of Doris's head had caught her, while she hastily scrabbled for her mobile with her other hand.

'We've gotta tell the coppers. Oh, God we've gotta tell them.' She nodded, wide eyed, at Doris.

Her face deathly white, Doris clutched her chest as she collapsed onto the pavement, and Sandra screamed again.

CHAPTER SIX

Alerted by the loud scream, as she was about to enter the newsagent's shop further along the main street where she now worked, Kerry Lumsdon looked quickly up the street just as Doris keeled over.

She blinked for a moment. Then, recognising Sandra, she knew who the person on the floor had to be. 'Shit, it's Doris.' Turning, she let the door slam shut, giving the five people inside a shock, then ran towards Sandra and Doris.

Kerry, her dark hair in a short bob, her dream of running one day soon for England coming closer by the month (she had already in the past year won every regional race she'd been entered for), took less than a minute to

41

cross the distance between them. Kerry's other dream of one day having something she could call breasts still hadn't happened – although, according to her tape measure last night, which she didn't believe, she was nearly half an inch bigger than a year and a half ago. Progress of a sort, I suppose, had been the thought going through her head just as she'd heard the scream.

When she reached them, Sandra was gently patting Doris's face. 'Come on, Doris. Stop pissing about and wake up, you're starting to freak me out now.'

'Is she all right?' Kerry dropped to her knees and looked at Sandra. 'Please say she's all right, Sandra. Please,' she begged.

The pure horror on Sandra's face made Kerry recoil for a moment. Then, expecting the worst, really wanting to put her hands over her eyes in case she saw what she was dreading, she looked down at Doris.

Kerry had known Doris all of her young life. Many a time Doris had fed her and her brothers and sisters when there had been no food in the house, even though a lot of the time she was hard up herself. Adding an extra couple of potatoes in the pan fed small kids well, she always said. She had even paid for school trips, when Kerry or one of the others had been the only kid in the class unable to afford it, all of them out of the goodness of her heart, when there was no money around – which had pretty much been a constant state of affairs in the Lumsdon household, because just about every week most of the money had been spent on the booze, by their mother Vanessa. As these thoughts rushed through Kerry's head, her heart rate sped up and her hands began to shake.

'Please ... please don't die, Doris.'

'No ... no, Kerry, please don't worry... I think she just fainted because ... because...' Sandra, whose own face was chalk white, swung her head towards the window.

Slowly. Kerry turned. It took a few moments for it all to sink in. Then she stared, open mouthed, in horrified fascination at the carnage, as the sound of sirens could be heard in the distance.

Sandra turned back to Doris. Could it be a heart attack, she wondered? The older woman was very quiet, and she looked so very pale.

'Surely if she's just fainted, she would be awake by now?' she muttered, her own heart fluttering in her mouth.

Kerry started to cry. 'Please say she's not gonna die, Sandra,' she pleaded.

'No, no.' Sandra put her hand on Kerry's arm. 'I told you, she just fainted.'

Kerry looked at her, disbelief written on her face.

CHAPTER SEVEN

Sanderson frowned down at the report in his hand, as he tapped the desk with his finger. The frown deepened the already heavy lines in his forehead. His face had a lived-in look, but it was also a face that comforted, and his boss DI Lorraine Hunt often used him to play the good cop when interrogating a suspect. He had a fondness for Lorraine who he had known since she'd been a child. He also had a fondness for dark grey suits and crisp white shirts, which he wore unbuttoned at the neck.

He knew the reg of the vehicle that had been used in the hit and run in the early hours of this morning, he was more than certain of that. He just couldn't for the life of him remember where the hell from.

He massaged his temples. His head was pounding as he put the report down and rummaged through his drawer for a couple of paracetamol. He'd left the party around ten last night, as his wife had her sister and her husband up from Wales for a week. Sanderson didn't like him very much, and thought Dirk to be a right prat. He guessed that Dirk's wife didn't like him very much either, because of the filthy looks she kept throwing at him. Sanderson prayed that this was not a testing of the water trip, to see if his wife's sister would be welcome if she left the prat. Dirk worked in insurance, and the last time they had met, the fool had bored him stiff. He groaned inwardly at the thought of being in the company of Dirk for a week, never mind the sister in law. It really pissed him. But yesterday, Sanderson had been told in no uncertain terms what would happen to him if he got drunk and showed his wife up. In fact she had quite graphically described what she would do to his balls with a piece of wire and a knife.

'It's not like I'm an aggressive drunk or anything,' he mumbled, throwing two of the tablets into his mouth and washing them down with a drink of cold tea. 'I just like to sing. Where's the harm in that?'

'Might be because you sound like a frog farting up a drainpipe,' Dinwall said, walking into the room. 'In fact, it's hard to tell who's the worst, you or Luke.'

Sanderson tutted. 'OK, gobshite, see if you know who this number plate belongs to. I know I've seen it before. It's right there on the tip of my tongue.'

'Well spit it out.' Dinwall grinned, then went on. 'Well, that's the mind for you, you see. Obviously, you don't really want to know who's it is do you.'

45

'I wish you'd stop reading all those daft psychology books along with your regular mumbo jumbo rubbish. I don't know what's worse the aliens, or the ghosts.'

'Aye, right.' Dinwall, casually dressed in jeans and green t-shirt, walked over to the desk and picked the report up. 'Aye,' he said without hesitation, 'it's Luke's.'

'What!'

'It's–'

'I know what you said, but it can't be.'

'How's that?'

'Because this is the car that was used in a hit and run in the early hours of this morning.'

'No way, man... Told you that you didn't want to know.' Dinwall nodded in a knowing way.

'The CT camera shows only one car passing through Houghton Cut around the time of the death, one thirty in the morning, and it's that one. Luke's.' Sanderson shook his head and sighed, his exasperation showing on his face. Sometimes, he thought, just sometimes he wanted nothing more than to punch Dinwall on his big nose – or better still, yank his stupid ponytail – and there was no time like now. He resisted the urge, even though his fingers were twitching.

Still staring at the report, Dinwall said, 'Shit... You seen him this morning?'

'No.'

'What about the boss?'

'She's not in either.'

Dinwall frowned. 'Haven't you tried phoning her?'

'Obviously,' Sanderson snapped, snatching the report out of Dinwalls hand.

'OK, OK. Don't go all touchy on me 'cause you had a pint or two last night and you're feeling the worse for it today. Not my fault you can't take your booze.'

'Has anyone ever...'

'What?'

'Never mind.'

Dinwall shrugged. 'Maybes Luke and the boss have took off for a bit. Weren't they talking of Paris or somewhere? They might have gone, and someone's nicked the car. It's not like both of them to be missing, this time on a morning, is it?'

'She would have phoned.'

'Whatever. But I bet the guys in traffic know who the car belongs to by now.'

'Hmm. Reckon they do. Better try the boss again.'

'Yeah well you do it 'cause I know she'll go friggin crazy.'

Sanderson frowned at him as he took his mobile out.

CHAPTER EIGHT

Santa took up his position across the road from the shop just as the ambulance and a police car arrived. A small gathering had built up, and most people were staring worriedly across the road.

'What's up here, like?' Santa asked the crowd in general.

'Looks like that big woman's collapsed or something,' an old man replied, as he lit a cigarette with shaking hands.

'Anyone know who she is?'

'Jesus, that's Doris Musgrove,' a woman in a tartan jacket said, looking at the people around her and nodding.

'That's Jacko's mother,' another said.

The crowd had now reached over twenty, and word rapidly spread from one to the other as the ambulance and the police car arrived simultaneously from different directions. A couple of mobile phones were pulled out and the message took fire. One phone was held aloft and its owner filmed everything, the camera recording all the details.

White faced, Sandra pointed with her finger to the window as a young officer jumped out of the police car and ran up to her.

Carter, with a feeling deep in his gut that he was going to regret this, followed Sandra's shaking finger with his gaze and swung his head to the window, while the ambulance crew quickly put Doris on a stretcher and transported her into the ambulance.

It took Carter a few moments to process exactly what he was seeing. 'Oh, dear God,' he muttered, as he moved towards the door. While Kerry, with Sandra's arm holding her up, vomited into the gutter.

The door was unlocked, and opened easily with the faint ringing of tiny bells. As he stepped inside the cat flew past him, craving the freedom of outdoors or, Carter thought, terrified of what had gone on in here.

Carefully, he stepped inside. His stomach churned at the smell, making him feel sick, it smelled much like an abattoir he'd visited once with his lorry driver uncle as a child, a place he'd vowed never to go to again. There was blood splattered all over the walls, making large circular patterns as if it had been done deliberately, the floor had the same patterns but marred with paw prints. Gagging, he stepped back outside, it was obvious there was nothing he could do for the victim, and rather than contaminate the crime scene, he closed the door behind him and stood guard until the experts arrived.

Having phoned Jacko Musgrove and told

him about his mother, assured the ambulance staff that they were both all right, and told the police woman, who had arrived shortly after Carter, that they would both be available for questions later, Sandra took Kerry home.

Arm in arm, they walked up Kerry's path as doors started opening and curtains twitched up and down the street. Vanessa Lumsdon had been watching out of the window for them. She quickly opened the door as they reached it, and ushered Kerry and Sandra into the house.

Vanessa, a recovering alcoholic, had changed drastically in the past twelve months. Her skin was much clearer, her eyes brighter, and the natural flush on her cheeks had returned. Her brown hair shone and was tied up in a neat bun. She wore a pink blouse with jeans, and now looked nearer her real age instead of fifteen years older.

'So what happened? There's all sorts of rumours flying around the place already.'

Kerry, usually courageous, forthright and determined, despite the trauma of her sister's kidnapping a year ago, was shaken by her first real touch with death. She shook her head as a tear rolled down her cheek. 'I think she's dead, Mam... I think poor Doris is dead.'

'No,' Sandra said quickly, as Vanessa put her arm around Kerry, sat her down on the settee and sat next to her. Kerry grabbed hold of her mother and sobbed on her shoulder.

Vanessa frowned over Kerry's shoulder at Sandra.

Sandra shook her head. 'I think she's had some sort of heart attack from the shock of seeing the dead shopkeeper.'

Vanessa gasped. 'I didn't quite understand what you said on the phone. I...' She patted Kerry's back. 'I'm sure Doris will be all right, love.'

'Yes, Kerry, I'm certain it's just a mild one.' Sandra mentally crossed her fingers as she went on, 'They'll sort her out in the hospital. Don't worry. Doris is a tough old bird.'

'OK,' Vanessa said, as she squeezed Kerry's shoulder, 'I'll make us a cup of tea.'

She hurried into the kitchen, recently painted bright lemon by Vanessa's two sons, Robbie and Darren. Her hands were shaking as she spooned sugar into the cups. She'd already had one shock this morning. Her sixteen year old daughter Claire was supposed to be stopping out at a friend's overnight, the first time she'd stayed out for over a year since she'd been kidnapped. But when she'd phoned half an hour ago, it was to find out from the friend's parents that Claire had not stopped there at all. In fact, they hadn't seen Claire all week, and their own daughter had already left for school.

Vanessa had kept the news to herself as the other kids went on their way, the little ones to school in the care of Darren, and Kerry and Robbie to work. Robbie's new job as a farm hand on the local farm was one he really loved. Everything had been good when she had first woken up this morning, the best for years. 'And how quickly that can change,' she muttered.

She prayed that Doris would be all right. The kids loved her to bits. She bit her lip to stop the yearning. It was times like this when the picture of a bottle swam relentlessly into her mind.

'God!' She could actually taste the golden liquid pouring down her throat. She pulled in a deep breath.

It would make things so much easier. Her gut feeling was that today she was going to pay for the best year of her life.

Her right hand began to twitch, as she pictured a beautiful bottle of whiskey with her name on it.

'No.' She shook her head. And, 'No,' again as her chin set stubbornly.

She took a few more deep breaths to steady herself. Her daughter's needs were much greater than hers at the moment. She winced as she remembered a time when she probably wouldn't have given a toss about Kerry's needs – her own, and the guilt she had carried for years, had come way above any of her kids' needs for way too long. But all that had changed now. She was never going back to what she had been. No way! This she had promised, when Claire had been returned to them safe and well.

She picked the tray up and hurried back into the sitting room, pleased to see a little colour coming back into her daughter's face. The poor kid had been chalk white, and Sandra had been pretty much the same.

As she crossed the threshold, the sound of numerous sirens caused her to pause and frown at Sandra.

'What the–?' Sandra got up and looked out the window. 'It's a fire engine and a couple of cop cars, heading up Daffodil Close.'

'God, I hope nobody's hurt.'

'No ambulances yet.'

Vanessa put the tray down on the coffee table. Straightening up, she looked at her daughter and said, 'What a fucking day!'

CHAPTER NINE

Tugging at her light grey suit jacket and pulling the collar of her lemon blouse out from under her handbag strap, her hair scraped back from her face into a French plait, Lorraine scowled her way into the station. Those who knew her well took one look and gave her a wide berth. She reached her desk just as Sanderson, followed by Dinwall, came in.

'You seen Luke this morning, boss?' Sanderson asked.

Lorraine put her can of Diet Coke on her desk, and the frown deepened. 'That's a no. And can I tell by your face that you know something I don't?'

'Er ...no... That is... I might.'

'Stop pissing about, Sanderson, I'm not in the mood.'

Dinwall opened his mouth, but whatever he was going to say was frozen by an, 'I dare you to interrupt' stare from Lorraine. Swinging her head back to Sanderson, she demanded quickly, 'Well? Spill it!'

Sanderson took a deep breath, then said in a rush, 'It's, er ... I have been trying to phone you... It's Luke's car, boss. It was used in a hit and run in the early hours of this morning.'

'What?' She held her hand up quickly to stop Sanderson from repeating himself. 'No way mate. For fuck's sake, how could you even... Sanderson!'

'I don't boss, no no no! I'm just saying it's his car, that's all. I'm surprised you didn't know.'

'I forgot to put my phone on charge last night. Never heard the alarm, so got up late this morning, and the stupid phone was stone bloody dead. There might be something wrong with the damn thing, it seems to need charging up a lot lately. And Luke hasn't got a house phone. Says he can't see the point in having three phones in the house.'

She took her phone out of her bag and plugged it in to the wall socket behind her desk, then turned back to Sanderson. 'How serious a hit and run?'

'Fatal.'

'Shit!'

'Where is he?' Dinwall, lover of gossip, asked, one eyebrow arched in a question.

Lorraine slowly shook her head. 'He didn't come home last night. And when I find him, he is so gonna wish he had.' Her words, quietly spoken, were for Sanderson, an old and very trusted friend whom Lorraine had always seen as a father figure.

Dinwall raised his eyebrows, and was about to leave the room when Lorraine snapped, 'Just where do you think you're going, motor mouth?'

'Er, nowhere, boss.'

'Dead right. Until I find out just what the hell is going on, we keep this to ourselves. And if I want your opinion, trust me – I will give it to you.'

Hiding a smile, Sanderson nodded. 'Don't worry, Lorraine. There'll be some rational reason.'

'Yeah, gotta be,' Dinwall put in, looking from one to the other while nodding his head.

'So who was the last of the stag party to see Luke last night?'

Sanderson shrugged. 'I left around ten o'clock.'

'Actually, I think Luke went about five minutes before we all left,' Dinwall said.

'On his own?'

He shrugged. 'Think so. We were all a bit smashed by then. One minute he was there, the next he was gone. Actually, come to think of it, he didn't look too well. He sort of kept swaying about the place. Seemed like one minute he was stone cold sober, and the next minute he was practically mortal drunk.'

'Strange. Are you sure he was drunk?' Lorraine frowned, knowing that Luke was far from a drinker.

'Actually, now I think about it – yeah, he was. What else could it have been? I mean, he certainly looked and acted drunk, and actually the last thing... I'm sure I heard him ask for more.'

Sanderson looked at Dinwall and shook his head. 'He wasn't drunk when I left at ten. I've never really seen Luke drunk. He had a couple of glasses of water between. He also had a glass of orange juice, now I remember.'

'So he wasn't drunk at ten o'clock?' Lorraine asked.

Dinwall shrugged as Sanderson shook his head.

'Actually...' Dinwall started to say but was cut short by Lorraine.

'What the fucking hell is with all the "actually"? This "actually," and that "actually". Just discovered the flaming word, have we?'

'Sorry. boss. The brain's actu ... a bit slow this morning.'

'This morning? Huh.'

Loving it, Sanderson beamed at Lorraine, but she was looking out of the window lost in thought for the moment.

So what the hell happened between ten and half past eleven? Lorraine sighed. How the hell am I gonna find out, when the only sober one left the pub at ten, and the rest were blind fucking drunk?

'So, Sanderson – who was mown down by the car?'

'A teenage girl. Her body was found in the middle of the road. She, er... She had been run over more than once. The car that knocked her down reversed over her again, then whoever it was took off and just left her there.'

'So we're talking murder.'

Slowly Sanderson nodded. 'Looks like it.'

Just then Lorraine's supervisor came in. By

the grim look on his face, Lorraine guessed the news was not good.

Reading her face, he said, 'So, you've finally heard.'

She nodded. 'Sorry, phone wasn't charged. And I don't know where he is. And there's no way on earth Luke would be capable of doing something like this. I know it, and you know it. So why didn't someone come and get me? Better still, why wasn't someone pounding on the door for Luke?'

'Not a lot you or anyone could have done Lorraine. Believe it or not, it took them a while to trace the owner. Apparently a couple of networks were down due to the weather, plus the road to Durham was cut off for a couple of hours, due to the heavy snow. The night shift dealt with it the best they could, which basically meant erecting a tent, and standing guard over the body until the weather eased off.'

Lorraine looked out the window. The sun was shining now. Until you looked at the ground and saw the patches of snow, you would think it was a summer's day, except it was damn cold.

'Anyhow, for what it's worth, I don't think Luke had anything to do with it, either. Nor does anyone else here. But as the law stands, at this moment he's the prime suspect.'

Lorraine felt her knees weaken, and reached out her right hand to her chair to steady herself. Dinwall quickly moved forward and pulled the chair round for her to sit on.

'No way.' Shaking her head she quickly sat down.

'I'm sorry, Lorraine, there's not a person I know who doesn't agree, but you know the rules.'

She glared up at him. 'You know it wasn't Luke.'

'As I said, no one believes Luke had anything to do with it. But there is a procedure we must put in place, to protect us and Luke.'

'We have to find him,' she muttered, more to herself than the officers in the room. 'There's got to be an explanation for this.' She banged her fist on the table, scattering the files she'd been looking at. 'For God's sake, he could be lying anywhere seriously hurt.'

Clark exchanged a sympathetic look with Sanderson, before going on. 'I'm really sorry, Lorraine, but you're not on the case. You're too involved.'

'What?' Lorraine glared at him.

'I don't want you anywhere near this. Obviously we'll keep you up to date and informed, but other than that, it's hands off. And I mean it, totally.' He put his hand on her shoulder. 'We'll get to the bottom of it, don't worry. In the meantime, I think it's best that you stay well away from this case and concentrate on the shop murder.'

'No, I can't. This is Luke, for God's sake!'

'It's an order.' He turned and left the room.

'Fuck!'

'It's obvious that Luke's car was stolen,' Sanderson said.

'Aye, but where the hell is he? And where's the car?' She stood and moved to the window.

'Why don't you go and get yourself home, Lorraine. I'll phone you if he turns up here.'

'How can I? There's the new murder case up at Houghton.'

'You don't think they're connected?' Dinwall asked. 'I mean,' he shrugged knowing he was digging a deep hole, but unable to stop himself.

Lorraine gave him a look that would have frozen water in a boiling kettle. She refastened her jacket and picked up her bag, swallowed the last of her Diet Coke, threw the can into the bin and said, 'Best I get up to the shop, see what's going on there. From what I've heard, it's pretty gruesome. In the meantime, Sanderson, if Luke shows up, tell him he'll be wishing he was dead when I finally get to see him.'

'Oh, I will that.' Sanderson and Dinwall both stepped to one side as she stomped past them.

'Go easy on the lad, boss. You know he's

not a drinker,' Dinwall said to her retreating back. 'Urgh!' He grunted as Sanderson dug him in his ribs with his elbow. 'Just saying, like.'

Lorraine tossed her head as she left them and went to her car.

CHAPTER TEN

Darren Lumsdon had shot up over the last year, easily growing a good six inches. Like his sister Kerry and brother Robbie, he had black hair, but that was where the resemblance ended. His eyes were brown, and his skin was a few shades darker than the rest of the family. Not that it bothered him, or any of his clan, nor the neighbourhood kids he'd grown up with. He'd put up with a bit of name calling from kids in different years at school, but that was few and far between. Like his big sister Kerry, he had big dreams. Football. He lived and breathed it.

And now he had a full new kit, and a pair of brand new boots. His school uniform was new and spotless. His Mam was getting better, much better – he felt like hugging himself with glee at the change in her. Robbie and Kerry both had jobs. And the best of it all... He had a game tonight where the Sunder-

land scout was coming, just to see him play.
Things that didn't seem possible a year ago
were finally beginning to happen. Good
things that had happened to other people,
but not somebody like him.

Somebody from nowhere.

His body thrummed with excitement, and
he knew he was grinning like a raving idiot as
he walked towards the school gates, after
dropping his sisters off at their school just
down the road. But he couldn't help it, it was
all he could do to stop himself from jumping
up and punching the sky time and time
again. He couldn't ever remember in his
whole life feeling so good, so, so fantastic.

What if I actually make it as a professional
footballer?

Oh God!

Me... Darren Lumsdon.

The kid from nowhere!

He pictured himself running the length of
the whole pitch and scoring for Sunderland,
and the whole crowd going mad and shouting his name over and over.

He burst out laughing as he dashed tears
of joy from his face, remembering what
Jacko Musgrove had told him more than
once: 'The sky's the limit, kid.'

And it was, and didn't it feel good. He
laughed again, then looked around, in case
someone had heard him laughing.

Great. No one there. Don't want locking

up in the nut house before I even get me chance.

Today is the best day of my life.

But best get a move on, he thought, I'm the last one in again. If Frosty Foster catches me, he'll be on me case all day. He shook his head, wondering again what the old twat of a history teacher had against him.

Quickly, he moved towards the school gates. He was about to pass through when someone wearing jeans and a light brown hoodie stepped in front of him.

Darren took a step back as the hoodie shoved his hood back, revealing the mean scowling face of someone in his early twenties. Dark haired, blue eyed, but with very pale skin. About to take another backward step, Darren was suddenly pushed forward from someone behind him until he was nose to nose with the stranger.

'What the–?' His heart sinking back to its usual place of rock bottom, Darren stared in fear at his attacker. As the best day of his life began to slowly spiral into the worst day of his life.

CHAPTER ELEVEN

'Can somebody do something with that flaming cat? It's sitting out there, covered in blood,' Lorraine said, stepping under the tape and into the shop. 'We'll have the RSPCA on our backs next. More friggin' forms to fill in.'

'They've been called, boss,' Carter said.

'I should hope so. But in the meantime, Carter, catch it, wash it, and friggin' well feed it... And be careful – we don't want any reporters snapping pictures of you being made a fool of by a flaming cat.'

'Yes, boss.' Carter hurried back outside, while Lorraine studied the crime scene. The floor was sticky with blood that surrounded the body in an almost perfect semicircle. And the blood on the walls looked suspiciously as if it had been put there on purpose. She glanced at the body, wondering if it had been drained of blood. It was then she realised that nothing would surprise her. The world was getting worse by the day. She rubbed her temples, the beginning of a headache just behind her eyes.

'Where the fuck are you?' she muttered to

herself, for the hundredth time that morning.

A few minutes later, Carter was back, minus the cat.

Lorraine was staring at her phone, praying it would ring, or at the very least deliver a message from Luke, but once again the screen was blank. Shoving it back in her pocket, she looked up at Carter. 'Well?'

'It just keeps moving, boss. When I step back, it moves back to where it was before, and when I step forward, it moves back. If you know what I mean.'

'So the cat is literally taking the piss out of you?'

Carter's face reddened.

'Don't you know anything about animals, Carter?'

He shook his head. 'My mother's allergic to most of them. I never had a pet, boss.'

Lorraine sighed. 'Food, Carter, food. That'll do it every time. There must be something in that tiny kitchen out back – that's assuming the cat does belong to the victim, although the way it's hanging around, it probably does. Try not to disturb anything, Carter, and as quick as you can, please. I'm sick to death of seeing people pointing at it. One woman just vomited over the wall, for God's sake.'

'Yes, boss.' Carter went into the back room. It had recently been painted white and turned into a kitchen cum office. The sky blue curtains at the window were closed, so Carter flicked the light switch on.

After a quick look round, he took the few steps needed to the sink and opened the cupboard door. He grinned as he picked up a box of cat treats and hurried back into the shop.

'Got them, boss.' He triumphantly waved the box in the air. 'Oh – hi, Scottie.' He had just noticed the pathologist, who was standing next to Lorraine.

Scottie, dark haired, tall and of stocky build, smiled at Carter and said, 'For the cat, or you?'

'Funny.' Carter glanced at Lorraine.

'Go get it, Carter.'

When he'd gone out of the door, Scottie said, 'Has he made his mind up yet?'

'About?' Lorraine raised one eyebrow.

'Come on, kiddo. Don't tell me you don't know what I'm on about, you're far from green.'

Lorraine, her mind split in two with worry for Luke and various thoughts about the murder victim, snapped, 'Will you for God's sake get to the point?'

Scottie raised his eyebrows at her tone but, having heard about Luke over the grapevine, forgave her immediately. He heaved a deep sigh and said, 'Has the lad made his mind up if he's in love with you, or Luke?'

'What!'

'Jesus, Lorraine.' He stared at her for a moment. 'You really haven't noticed, have you?'

'Er ... noticed what?'

'The way the poor lad is torn between the pair of you. Me, my money's on Luke.'

'Don't tell me they're taking bets.'

Scottie grinned, then shrugged.

'Dinwall!'

Scottie shrugged again, his whole frame moving this time as he tried to keep the laugh in.

'It is him, isn't it?'

'I'm saying nowt.'

'Oh yes, you are.' Lorraine put her hands on her hips and stared at him.

Scottie folded at once. 'OK, yes. It was Dinwall's idea to take bets. But surely you must have seen it coming?'

Lorraine shook her head. She didn't have time for this, and now her mind really was in a whirl. 'Look, whatever Carter's sexuality is, it's his business and no one else's. OK?'

And yes, she thought. I did wonder, and I'm not surprised.

'Here.' She took her purse out of her bag, pulled a ten pound note out, and handed it to Scottie. 'Put a tenner on it being Luke.'

Laughing, Scottie took the money.

'Under a pseudonym, of course.'

'Of course.'

CHAPTER TWELVE

Jacko stared at his mother. Her face was grey, although she never really had much colour, so that could be nothing. But it was the machines that they had her hooked up to that were depressing him. He clenched his fists. He had not stopped praying since he'd found out what had happened. His first instinct had been to go and get his daughter out of school, but thankfully Mr Skillings had talked him out of it. He'd been right in saying there was no need to alarm Melanie until they knew the true facts.

The old man was down the hallway trying to work the coffee machine. From the time he was taking, Jacko guessed he was having some bother.

'How the hell am I gonna tell Melanie if ... if...' he whispered to himself. 'Please, Mam, wake up. Dear God, please make her wake up.'

Mr Skillings limped in just then, his walking stick tapping on the floor, with a strange teenager in tow carrying a dark blue plastic tray with two coffees on. Standing still, Mr Skillings raised his stick and gestured towards the bedside cabinet with it. 'Put them on there, son, and thank you very much.'

The boy, blond and around fifteen years old, nodded shyly at Jacko, who smiled and nodded back to him, thinking of his Mam telling him the other day about two lovely girls giving up their seats on the bus for her and Mr Skillings. 'A rare event,' she'd said, 'which proves that not all teens are bad. They just get a bad press.' The boy left, and Jacko breathed in the smell of coffee.

As he reached for one of the cups, Mr Skillings said, 'I was wondering if I should phone Dolly, in case...'

Jacko looked up at him. Not wanting to meet his eyes, thinking he'd handled that very badly, Mr Skillings quickly swung his head to the window. Jacko swallowed hard, and sighed before saying, 'No. Don't disturb her holiday. Mam's gonna be just fine.'

Looking back at the silent woman in the bed, Mr Skillings doubted that very much.

CHAPTER THIRTEEN

Luke opened his eyes and blinked rapidly for a moment. He realised that he was star-ing at the sky, he had a pounding headache, and felt sick as a dog. He struggled to sit up, to the sound of dozens of small falling rocks, and the screeching sound of seagulls. 'Where the hell...?'

Wherever he was it was high, very high, and very cold. Slowly he moved his left hand. Suddenly there was nothing there, his fingers, scrabbling around, finding nothing but empty space. And again the sound of more falling rocks, which he had obviously dislodged.

Shit, he thought. Where the hell am I?

His heartbeat quickened as his mind came up with a possible answer, and in fear he rejected it at once. Ever so slowly, he turned his head to the left and gasped, his heart somersaulting in shock, as he realised instantly from the fantastic view that there was only one place he could be – unless he'd been transported over night to Penshaw Monument.

'Table Rock,' he muttered. 'How the hell...?'

Table Rock was a huge outcrop of magnesium limestone, a well known landmark that guarded the entrance to Houghton le Spring. From its height, the whole of the Durham valley and beyond could be seen.

He started to shiver and, staring in horror at the edge of the rock, ever so slowly dusted the snow from his body. An inch at a time, he edged away from danger. Just a foot from the edge, and still not feeling safe enough, he had to stop as he vomited the entire contents of his stomach into the snow. Groaning, he wondered how he had got here, and why the hell he couldn't remember it. All he could think of was that he'd been carried here and placed on the edge by someone. But there definitely had to be more than one person involved, unless the guy was superhuman.

'The bastards thought I'd fall over the edge. Damn miracle that I haven't.' Then he panicked again, and reached inside his pocket for his wallet.

'Shit,' he said a moment later, then he started coughing, when the coughing subsided he quickly checked for his car keys and his phone. All were missing. 'Fairly been rolled. Bastards. What the fuck happened?'

The very last memory he had was of finding himself in the middle of Houghton. Slowly he went through everything that had happened the night before. After a moment, he remembered the three youths, how they had all but sat on his knee.

'It has to be them, bastards. They must have spiked my drink. God knows they were close enough. But why?' He glanced to the left of him again, and came to the conclusion that there was only one reason. Somebody wanted him dead... But why?

Shivering, he slowly rose to his feet, trying to ignore the smell of the vomit, which covered his t-shirt and jacket. Luke was a very fit man and worked out frequently, but a night on stony ground takes its toll, especially in the snow. Plus, his face – particularly his nose – was killing him. Tenderly, he touched the soreness, and his fingers came away covered in blood. His nose also felt twice the size it should be, and he realised that his right eye was nearly swollen shut. 'Gotta get off of here. Gotta get home. Right now. Lorry will be worried sick.'

Shaking his head, and then holding it in his hands to stop the spinning, he muttered, 'Don't do that again.'

Slowly he turned right and headed off the rock, having to stop every few minutes to cough and get his breath back. Finally he made it through the fields to Grasswell.

He had to stop and sit on the seat outside the bus stop, across the road from the fish shop, knowing he could go no further unless he crawled. Ignoring the strange looks he was getting from the couple who, thinking he was a drunk, quickly passed by, then he spotted someone he knew. The pain in his neck was so intense now that he couldn't help but drop his head onto his chest. Fearing that the man would walk past like the couple had, he waved his arm feebly in the air, managing a very weak, 'Hi... Hi.'

Len Jordan, out for a walk with his greyhound Meg, stopped and looked Luke up and down. 'Bloody hell, mate, what happened to you?'

Luke slowly lifted his head and mumbled. 'Don't know ... only, only just sort of come round. You.' He paused, trying to catch a breath. 'You were in the Beehive last night... Did you ... see anything strange going on?'

'Not that I can remember, but I think you best be getting home, mate. Your clothes look soaked through, your face is a mess and you'll catch your death if you're not careful. Plus I can smell you from here.'

'Yeah, see you.' Luke struggled to stand.

'No, no, sit back down. I'll go and get the car. It's gonna piss down any minute, and I think you're in need of a doc.'

Feeling helpless and unable to do anything for himself, Luke fell back onto the seat.

'Two minutes, OK?' Len hurried off.

He had only just crossed the road when Len saw his cousin Danny driving his van towards him. Jumping onto the road and waving his arms in the air, he flagged him down.

'What the fuck? You trying to get yourself killed, you fucking lunatic?' Danny yelled, screeching to a halt.

'It's that copper, Luke Daniels. The black one. He's in a bad way. The poor bugger needs a lift home.'

'Call the fucking coppers, then.'

Len frowned at him. 'Not funny. You gonna

73

help, or what?' With a sigh, Danny said, 'I suppose so. Hoy the ugly mutt in the back, and jump in.'

Len frowned at him.

'I mean the fucking dog.'

It took both of them to lift Luke, who was barely conscious now, into the van. After a lot of pulling and pushing, they finally had him in and strapped up.

'I think we should call an ambulance, Len. This bugger's in a really bad way, mate. He's either had a hell of a fall, or some bastard's fairly beaten him up. And he fucking stinks to high heaven... Jesus Christ.'

'Nah.' Len shook his head. 'Probably just can't handle his drink. And I'm guessing he wouldn't want his copper mates to see him like this. Anyhow, it would take more than one to beat him up, mate, he's a big bugger. You didn't see him that night at Houghton Feast last year when he collared that perve who'd been following those girls and then tried it on with him. Knocked seven kinds of shite out of him, he did.'

'Home,' Luke muttered, then started sneezing.

'See!'

'OK. Have it your way.'

Reaching Luke's house just before the heavens opened to a torrential downpour, which quickly washed away all traces of the snow, Luke remembered he didn't have his

74

keys. 'Shit. Should have headed straight for the station.'

'What you say?' Len asked, moving his head closer to Luke's. Luke's voice had been little more than a murmur.

Unable to reply, Luke began to shiver. Quickly it got worse, but instead of feeling cold, he felt strangely hot. He wiped the sweat off his forehead as they helped him out of the van.

'You really sure you don't want me to call a doctor?' Danny asked again.

'No.' Luke leaned over the small wall between his house and next door's, and knocked feebly on the door, praying old Rosie was in and not out walking her little yorkie, Beth.

'No keys,' he managed to whisper, when Danny and Len both gave him inquisitive looks.

Thank God, he thought as her door slowly opened, and heaving a sigh of relief he muttered, 'Something right at last.'

'What's the matter, love?' Rosie asked. Before he could say anything, she yelled, 'Oh my God, you're a right mess. Come on in, quick, the rain's getting heavier.'

Helped by Len on one side and Danny on the other, Luke moved slowly back down his path, every bone in his body screaming, blood, snot and sweat mixed with rainwater dripping off his face. Halfway up Rosie's path, he stopped. That was it. He had no energy left to give. Slowly his knees buckled, and Rosie hurried out to help them.

CHAPTER FOURTEEN

Vanessa made an excuse to go into the kitchen where, with shaking hands, she took her mobile out. She glanced at it quickly then, with a heavy sigh, shoved it back into her pocket. Still no message from Claire.

And the little sod has ignored all of my calls. Just wait until I get my friggin' hands on her.

Vanessa wanted to slam the phone on the floor and stamp on it, as hard as she could, but that would mean she had lost control, and no way could she afford do that. To lose control meant she might reach for her old friend the bottle, then everything she'd worked for over the last year would be wasted.

It had taken months for the longing to subside, and even now she still felt the need on occasion – when the kids acted up, which to be honest wasn't that often, they were pretty good kids. God only knows how, after everything I put them through.

'Poor sods,' she muttered. 'Thank God for

our Robbie and Kerry.'

She grasped the edge of the table. Inside she felt as if her whole body was shifting from side to side. She'd tried to describe it as more of a lurch, but few people understood. She breathed deeply, gripping the table to stop her hands from searching for something, anything to take the agony away. After a few minutes she felt better.

Thank God that now she was much stronger than she had ever been, for as long as she could remember. Each day had been a milestone in her battle. Her family and friends, especially Sandra, had helped her so much. Even strangers at the meetings had been so kind, but they knew what she was going through.

The secrets she'd kept for years had weighed heavy on her. They had finally come home to roost a year and a half ago, and boy, did they have a sting in their tail. A sting that had affected all of them. But hopefully it was all over now. Looking out the window, she sighed, thinking back to what had been, and what might have been.

She insisted that the girls carry their mobiles wherever they went. The cheap second-hand one Robbie had got for Claire might not be the height of fashion, but it was the link to her daughter that she so much needed.

'Little bitch,' she muttered. 'Where the

hell are you?'

'What's that you said, Mam?' Kerry came into the kitchen carrying the empty teacups.

'Oh, nothing,' Vanessa said quickly.

Far too quickly for Kerry's liking. She looked at her mother with suspicion. So far as she knew, her mother had not had a relapse, although the people at AA had said she may well do, and that if she did, they had to support her through it. Was this going to be the start?

'Are you sure?'

'Yes, why?'

'Thought I heard you talking to yourself.'

Vanessa laughed. 'Don't we all, now and again?' The last thing Vanessa wanted was for Kerry to be worrying about her sister, not until they at least knew what was up with Doris, and if the poor old bugger was going to be all right. She hoped and prayed that she herself was worrying for nothing.

Before Kerry could reply, the back door opened and Jill Fairbanks popped her head round. In her late twenties, and after numerous failed romances, Jill still lived with her parents, a few doors down from Vanessa. Her dyed blonde hair was cut in a short bob, and as always she was dressed in denim, denim and even more denim. 'Have youse lot heard about that bit lassie up on Houghton Cut?' she said, as her skinny body followed her head round the door.

78

Houghton Cut, the main road from Durham to Sunderland, was created in the Napoleonic Wars by French prisoners, as an easy route to transport troops from Durham to Sunderland. It was within walking distance of Table Rock.

Vanessa and Kerry looked at each other, as Sandra, hearing Jill's voice and sensing a bit of gossip, came into the kitchen.

'What's up, like?' she asked.

'Well!' Satisfied that she had everyone's attention, Jill went on, 'There's been a body found through the night. Apparently, it's a young lass.'

Vanessa gulped. 'How ... how young of a lass?'

'Dunno. Somebody said sixteen, somebody else said fifteen.'

Vanessa's body made a sickening thud as she hit the floor.

CHAPTER FIFTEEN

'Come on, Sanderson, give me a reason. A reason why some sick bastard would murder this particular young girl, and so fucking brutally.'

She needed Sanderson to kick her mind into work, and stop her constantly worrying about Luke.

Sanderson shrugged, as Dinwall came in with two coffees and a can of Diet Coke for Lorraine.

'She's pissed someone off,' Dinwall said, handing Lorraine her Coke.

'Obviously,' she snapped. Her mind still refusing to let go of the missing Luke, she opened the can and drank, thinking, where the hell are you, Luke? Where are you? Her heart sinking, she sighed as she put the can on her desk.

Patrols had been sent out, but so far no success. The landlord at the Beehive had said he had no recollection of hearing a car starting as he locked up, and couldn't swear if Luke's car had even been in the car park last night.

'Could be a random.' Sanderson said, reaching his hand out for his coffee, and nodding a 'Thank you' towards Dinwall. He sprinkled extra sugar in. Seeing that Lorraine was barely listening, he was about to repeat his statement when Lorraine snapped into the present.

'God, I so hope not.' She said. Random meant they could have a serial killer on their hands, and God only knew when he would strike again. They needed it to be someone the poor girl knew. A jealous boyfriend, a hated family member, again with a jealousy motive, or wanting something kept hidden, a secret the girl knew about.

'Has Carter managed to trace any of the girl's family yet, Dinwall?'

Dinwall frowned. 'Which case we talking about here?'

Lorraine shrugged. 'The teenager.'

'Right, that's a no. And no local missing teenage girls have been reported over the last twenty-four hours. Also,' he shook his head, 'you know that you aren't supposed to even be thinking about that case, boss.'

'She could be from further afield,' Sanderson said, as he shook his head at Dinwall.

'Correct. Dinwall get whoever is working this to widen the scope. In reality, she could have come from anywhere.'

He nodded, then coffee in hand, left to go into the communications room. The message, however, he never passed on. Detective Inspector Alison Fyfe and Lorraine had never once seen eye to eye. Surprisingly, he could on a rare occasion keep his mouth shut – plus he did not at all fancy being the messenger here, as Fyfe would definitely shoot him down, then probably go shit hot upstairs to complain about Lorraine meddling in her case.

He threw Fyfe a quick smile as he walked over to the computer bank, which she did not return. Instead she frowned, and he could feel her dark eyes boring into his back. Tall and slim, her dark hair cropped short, rumour had it that Fyfe had got where she was not through hard work or being a brilliant detective. The fact that she was having an affair with one of the high-ups was common knowledge.

Dinwall had a few words with one of the computer guys he knew well, then, still feeling Fyfe's eyes boring into his neck, he headed back to Lorraine's office.

Sanderson was sitting on the edge of the desk. 'Lorry, I wouldn't worry too much. Knowing Luke, he probably had more drink than he's used to, and my guess he'll be sleeping it off somewhere nice and cosy.'

'You think so?'

'I do. Have you tried ringing your mother?'

'Yeah, no flaming answer.'

Then for a moment, Lorraine's eyes lit up. Why the hell haven't I tried again. Luke and Mam get on really well, he even gets on with the wicked godmother. Bet the bugger has slept it off there, being molly cuddled by the Hippy and the Rock Chick – neither of whom bothered to phone me.

With a rising heart, she grabbed her phone and rang her mother's number. It was answered after three rings. 'Hello,' Peggy said.

'Oh, it's you.'

'And good morning to you too, Lorry.'

Lorraine pulled a face at Sanderson, before going on. 'Sorry, Peggy. Is Mam there?'

'You just missed her. She's gone to that

new farmer's market in Durham when I really need her here an'all...' She groaned as if she was in pain, then went on. 'I think I've sprained my ankle, it's all swollen, that's why I didn't go, even though I wanted to. The pain, oh my God, you wouldn't believe it.'

'Pain killers.'

'Tried the lot. Nothing seems to work.'

'Doctors.'

'Well...'

Suspecting another long drawn out debate on Peggy's ankle, Lorraine quickly said, 'OK, Peggy, I've got to go now.'

'Oh ... anything I can do, love?'

Lorraine took the phone from her ear and looked at it with a suspicious frown. The only time Peggy called her 'love' was when she wanted something.

'OK. Have you seen Luke at all?'

'Why? Don't tell me you've lost the gorgeous hunk?'

'Peggy... Have you seen him?'

'No.'

'Right, I'll er ... catch you later.'

'Something wrong, Lorry?'

'No ... no, nothing to worry about. Gotta go now. Bye.' She put the phone down before Peggy could tie her up with a hundred useless questions, and try to persuade her into whatever it was she wanted.

'No joy there, then,' Dinwall stated.

83

Lorraine sighed. 'I don't know what else to do.'

'Well, the uniforms are still out scouring the place.'

'What if he doesn't want to be found?'

'Have you any reason, any at all, to think that?'

Lorraine shook her head. 'Apart for a small ... no, not even small ... tiny row over Christmas baubles.' Lorraine shrugged. 'We hardly argue over anything.'

'Has he been himself lately?'

'I think I would have noticed if there was something wrong, Sanderson. I am after all a fucking detective.'

'Ah, but a lot of people don't realise that sometimes it's the closest to us that don't notice,' Dinwall said.

'You're sounding off again with your bloody psychology.' Sanderson frowned at him.

Putting her elbows on the desk and intertwining her fingers, she rested her chin on them. 'What we gonna do, Sandy?'

Seeing her eyes shining with unshed tears, he squeezed her shoulder. 'Just stop worrying Lorraine, I still say that he's sleeping it off somewhere.'

CHAPTER SIXTEEN

'I'm all right, how many bloody times do I have to tell you? Jesus!' Doris swung her legs off the bed. 'I'm going home, Doctor, and no if's or but's about it.' She reached for her coat, her face set in stubborn, don't mess with me lines.

The doctor, a large man with rolls of fat around his neck and tiny piercing black eyes, whose white coat was far too tight for him, looked to Jacko for support.

With a sigh, Jacko said, 'Mother, come on now. The doc only wants you to stay in overnight for observation. You know that... Better to be safe than sorry, that's what you always say, isn't it?'

'No way mate. I haven't even got so much as a stitch in me flaming head, have I? Flaming National Health, can't even afford to put a plaster on.' Without waiting for the doctor or Jacko to comment, she went on. 'Anyhow, it's just a tiny little bump, that's all. Flaming hell, I've had a lot worse than this and never clapped eyes on a doctor. Not, I might add, that I would ever get a chance to see one these days. I remember my friend Dolly wasn't too well six months ago, and she was told to make an appointment for three weeks later, would you believe! Bloody stupid, if you ask me.'

Jacko shuffled his feet in embarrassment as she went on. 'Doctors! All the flaming same the bloody lot of you. Before you know it, they've got you hooked on something or the other, and they'll be peddling their legal drugs.'

'Mother!'

'One drug for the bump on the head, and then another to take away the side effects of the first, and so on and so on. Well, this lady ain't no addict, OK? Never have been, never will be. Nor am I a flaming pincushion, right?' She stared down at her hand. 'Get this thing off me.'

'Mother, that's nonsense, and you know it. There are people alive today who would never have survived twenty years ago, if it wasn't for certain tablets.'

The doctor nodded his head, agreeing with Jacko.

'Don't look so flaming smug, mister, 'cause he knows nowt.' She jerked her head in the direction of Jacko.

He stood and shrugged at the doctor, trying to hide a smile because he knew he was on the losing side. Once his mother had made her mind up, nothing would or could shift her. He was pleased that she definitely seemed like her old self. 'Well, you did say you couldn't find anything wrong, Doc, and it was all probably down to shock.'

'Shock!' Doris almost yelled. 'Wouldn't you be in shock if you saw what I did?' Without waiting for either of them to answer, she thrust her hand at the doctor. 'Any time soon, please.'

'OK. On your head be it.' He blinked quickly, realising what he'd said, then looked at her hand as if it was beneath him to take the cannula out. 'I'll send a nurse in, and you'll have to sign the consent forms.'

'Anything to get me outta here. I'll even sign it in blood.'

Shaking his head, but relieved that his mother was perfectly all right, Jacko helped her with her coat and persuaded her to sit down until the nurse arrived. Reluctantly, and with much moaning, Doris did so.

Jacko walked over to the window and looked across the car park, mulling over Danny Jordan's latest money making scam. At first, Jacko had been more than a little unsure. Dressing up as a bunch of Santas on Christmas Eve, singing *Jingle Bells?* 'God, I can just picture it,' he muttered.

'Picture what?' Doris asked.

'Nowt, Mother.'

Got a fair pair of lugs on her, all right. He turned back to the window. And to pretend we're collecting for a charity is a little below the belt. But, as Danny had explained, no one was going to get hurt, and people would feel good helping out on Christmas Eve. They were bound to make a fortune at the Metro Centre this close to Christmas.

Because he'd given most of his winnings to his mother, Jacko had tried a few other gambling ways to win more money, only it hadn't worked. Fool that he was – there was no such thing as a winning streak, everything was random. He should have just kept to his regular bets. And, though not quite broke, he did need a cash injection, and pretty soon. He looked over at his mother, who seemed deep in thought staring at the far wall.

'No way,' he muttered, too low for her to hear. Can't remember her being so happy in a long time as when I gave her the money. No filling the sharks' pockets this Christmas from the Musgrove's, and that's a fact. And most of it will go on Melanie anyhow.

God, she'll be so happy when she sees her laptop.

He sighed. Although it goes way against the grain, guess I'm gonna have to dress up as a friggin' Santa Claus. He shook his head. The kids will probably think I'm a pirate Santa.

The nurse arrived then to take Doris's cannula out. She tried, but for a moment only, to get Doris to stay in the hospital. One look at her face and the nurse fell quiet.

'Thank you, dear,' Doris said with a charming smile, when the nurse was finished.

Jacko shook his head. Once his mother had got her own way, there was nobody sweeter.

'Come on, then, Mother. Let's hit the road.'

Pleased that his old friend was just fine, Mr Skillings followed them out, his cane tapping behind them. He had stood back and kept his own counsel for the last half hour, knowing far better than to interfere between mother and son, especially with Doris in the mood she was in.

As they left the hospital an ambulance, sirens screaming, pulled up to the hospital doors.

CHAPTER SEVENTEEN

'Boss,' Carter said from the doorway.

Lorraine looked up from the case files she had been going through, thinking (wrongly) that the paperwork would take her mind off the missing Luke. Not a chance. He was there every second. With a sigh she looked up. 'What is it, Carter?'

'It's old Rosie, boss, your neighbour, she's out the front. She wants to see you.'

Lorraine frowned. 'Whatever for?'

'Don't know, boss. When I asked, she said it was none of my business.'

'Yeah, that'll be Rosie all right... OK, Carter, tell her I'll be there in a minute.'

Carter nodded and closed the door behind him. Lorraine looked back at the folder, dated five years ago. She'd asked for anything around the country that referred to missing body parts. The folder in her hand fitted with this morning's murder only too well, along with five others. Somehow a tight lid had been kept on this spate of horrific murders, where each victim had been found with a knife in their back and a part of their body missing. The folders were on a need to know basis only.

She actually did know one of the detectives quite well, DI James Watson, who had been called into most of the murders, but it looked like he was no further forward, as the last case had been a year ago. Closing the top folder, she left her office and walked down to the front desk, wondering why Rosie was here, and thinking it could have something to do with Luke.

'Hello, Rosie,' she greeted the old woman, noticing the smell of lavender that always preceded her. Lorraine had been very surprised to find out from Selina that it was Luke who kept Rosie supplied in the stuff for birthdays and Christmas, and that every Thursday through the winter, Rosie made a big pan of ham broth and dumplings that Luke adored.

'It's your Luke, pet,' Rosie blurted out, before Lorraine had properly reached her. 'He's in the hospital, very poorly an' all, he is, God bless.'

'What?'

'Aye.'

'I mean, what's happened? Has he been in an accident?' Lorraine felt her heart beat speed up. She didn't know whether to be pleased that he'd turned up, or terrified in case he was seriously injured. Please, God, please. Let him be all right. She felt tears prick the back of her eyes, the word hospital whirring through her mind. They had checked all the hospitals in a twenty mile radius, no one of Luke's description had been brought in. Unless it had just happened.

'Please, Rosie.' She took a deep breath. 'Tell me exactly what happened.'

She took hold of the old woman's hand and looked into her eyes, fearing what she would see. But she had to know.

'Well, some blokes brought him home, he couldn't find his keys so I took him in, because he was in a right state, but after five minutes he was quite delirious, so I phoned the doctor, who sent for the ambulance. When it came, Luke kept mumbling something about Table Rock. I think by the state

91

he was in he might have been there all night, and the temperature he's running, wouldn't surprise me if the poor lad's got pneumonia.'

'God!'

'Now, Lorraine, I know you're concerned, but there's no need to blaspheme.'

Carter's jaw hung open in shock, as did the desk sergeant's. No one ever talked to the boss like that, if they wanted to get out alive. Quickly both of them swung their heads towards Lorraine, expecting an outburst.

But surprising them both, she put her arm across Rosie's thin shoulders, squeezed her and, with a smile, said, 'Thank you so very much, Rosie, for letting me know. I'll make sure you get a lift down home.'

'In a police car?'

'Sure, if that's what you want.'

Rosie's eyes shone with glee. 'Never been in a police car before... Oh, what will the neighbours think!' She grinned.

'Carter, take Rosie home, please. In fact, take the long way home.'

Rosie clapped her hands.

'Yeah, sure, boss.' Carter nodded at Rosie, then said to Lorraine, 'Er, will you let me know as soon as you hear anything, boss?'

'Of course,' Lorraine flung over her shoulder as she hurried back to her office for her bag.

After leaving instructions with the desk sergeant to alert everyone where she was going and to tell them about Luke, Lorraine hurried to the car pool, figuring if she used a police car, she would get there sooner.

So, she was thinking as she crossed the yard, he must have fallen down somewhere and spent the night out in the elements. Rosie's right, the daft sod probably has got pneumonia.

But you can recover from pneumonia easily enough in this day and age.

Can't you?

Course you can, miracles of modern science and all that.

He'll be all right.

I know he will.

As much as she tried to convince herself, there was still a niggle of doubt burrowing away in her mind. And she couldn't wait to be by his side.

CHAPTER EIGHTEEN

Martin Raynor took his headphones off and jumped quickly off his bed. The next moment he was standing behind his bedroom curtains, wondering if he dare peek out, and praying hard that if Stevie Masterton did come calling, his mother would remember to say that he was not in.

93

It had been real cool at first, a couple of years ago when Stevie had taken him under his wing, and to prove he was worth it he had done some things he wasn't proud of. Having been the victim of bullying all of his young life, it had been good when no one had dared say anything to him anymore, in case he told Stevie and they got a hell of a good thumping. But for the last six months, Stevie had been in jail after being caught red handed and locked up for burglary on a night Martin had come down with a flu virus. Not content with burgling one house, the idiot had actually done three in the same street. It had been third time unlucky, when he'd sneaked into a house where a bunch of heavies were playing cards. The word on the street was that the idiot had got what he deserved, a broken jaw and a broken leg, and many had laughed when told that he'd been left in a wheelie bin outside of the police station.

Martin had had a panic attack the next day, though, when he found out that Stevie had been caught in the act, thinking that he would most definitely have been with him and probably ended up in the same nick – he was already on a caution, through Stevie. The thoughts of being a gofer, for Stevie and anyone else in prison, had brought the panic attack on. His mother had panicked nearly as much as he, and rushed him to hospital. It

94

was there that one of the doctors passing him on the ward had stopped, stared at him for a moment, then come over and asked if he would like to try out a new cream for acne. And now his face was nearly clear, apart from a couple of spots in the corner of his mouth and another few on his chin.

He'd even got a job. Not much of a one, and the milkman who he delivered with wasn't holding out much hope for the future, as the milk round was decreasing weekly. 'Bloody supermarkets,' he said at least twenty times a day. The reason he'd set Martin on was as a favour to his mother, and the fact that he was getting too old to keep jumping in and out of the milk float.

All was going pretty good until yesterday when Stevie, fresh out of prison, had turned up with a new mate in tow. A mate Stevie had been banged up with. Stevie had been bad enough, but the guy who answered to Dev fairly terrified the life out of Martin, and the last twenty four hours had been worse than any nightmare. He'd felt sick as a dog last night, and doubted that he could take any more. He wanted out, but he could see no way. Everything was closing in on him. He wanted to bang his head against the wall, time and time again, until there was nothing left to think with. Sighing, he risked a quick glance out of the corner of the curtain.

Big mistake, he thought immediately, with a sinking heart, as he saw Dev standing at the gate grinning up at him. The next second there was a heavy thumping on the door.

'Shit, shit, shit.' He ran to the top of the stairs. 'I'll get it, Mam.'

His mother, on her way to the door, looked up the stairs at him. 'But I thought I was to say you weren't in.'

'Well, I'm in now, so just leave it, eh?'

'Make your bloody mind up, for God's sake,' she snapped at him. Shaking her head and muttering about crazy friggin' teenagers who could never make their minds up, she made her way back to the kitchen.

Taking a deep breath, Martin opened the door. Because he'd been seen, he'd had to dump plan A. Only there was no plan B. He could see himself being dragged back into the devious clutches of Stevie Masterton and his evil twin. Everything in front of him was leading to a huge black hole, and there was nothing to keep him from falling over the edge. What had happened last night had left him more than speechless. He'd screamed that much, his throat was still sore, plus pissing himself had only made the new guy laugh even louder.

He'd thought for a long time that Stevie was tainted with something bad, but Dev? Well, Dev was pure evil.

A moment later, he gasped in shock when

he was grabbed tightly by the scruff of his neck as Stevie, using his superior weight, forced him back against the door. 'You taking the fucking piss or what, mate?' He burst out laughing, and Martin knew he was remembering last night. 'Thought I told you to meet me up at the Blue Lion?'

'Sorr ... sorry. I was just gonna come, forgot what time yer said.' Martin had to force the words out. He managed, but in a very high pitched squeak.

Stevie let go of his throat. 'You sure about that?'

Wide eyed and terrified, Martin could only nod.

''Cause the new boss in there is asking especially for us. And our mate.' He thrust his head in the direction of Dev. 'Well, he's got plans an' all.'

Martin ran his tongue over his dry lips. 'So ... so who's the new boss, then?'

'Don't know, but whoever it is, they've got work for us. Come on.'

Stevie turned, and Martin closed the front door and shuffled down the path after him.

Another nightmare then. Seems every landlord in the Blue has to have a certificate in drug dealing, money laundering and whatever.

He sighed. What if I started to run and just kept right on going?

You wouldn't get anywhere, he answered

himself, as Dev slapped his shoulder.

'You weren't trying to fucking hide from us up there?'

'No,' Martin answered quickly. 'Why the fuck would I do that?' Inside he was shaking, and praying that Dev believed him. He'd tried his best to put a front on.

'Just a thought.' Dev shoved his fist under Martin's chin. ''Cause you can guess what would happen to you if you fucking tried any shit like that, can't you? And especially if you blabbed about last night.' He grinned, exposing a mouth filled with more than one rotten tooth, and Martin flinched at the smell.

Stevie laughed. 'Pissy Fartin' Martin.'

'Am I missing something?' Dev asked.

'That's his nickname. Fartin' Martin.'

Dev grinned. 'Wonder how you got that?' He punched Martin's arm.

Martin flinched. The blow had not been light. With a sinking heart, he fell in behind them as they headed up towards Houghton. He knew that he would lose his job. No way were these two ever gonna let him go. Stevie had threatened to hurt Martin's mother before he went into prison, saying it would all be his own fault if he didn't do what Stevie wanted him to do. Guess he'll follow through now – and if he doesn't, then that escapee from hell certainly will.

He looked under his eyelids at Dev's back.

Wonder what he was in jail for?

Something bad, that's a fact. I thought Stevie was a nut job, but I'm right – this twat's an evil fucker.

He shivered inside, wanting to run, but there was nowhere to run to.

I might as well be in jail. They'd catch me in two minutes. And if by chance they didn't, they know where I live.

And they knew his mother was there, all alone.

They reached the corner shop, and Dev turned around. 'Can of lager, now.'

'Yeah, I'll have one an' all.' Stevie grinned at him. 'Maybes two or three, Pissy Pants.'

'But I've got no cash.'

'So?' Dev raised his arms and shrugged.

Martin swallowed hard. Knowing full well what they meant, he backed away from them.

'You thinking of doing a fucking runner, Fartin'?' Dev asked, swaggering up to him.

'No,' Martin said quickly. But that was what he longed to do, what his body was screaming to do, as every muscle tensed so hard that they became a physical pain. 'I've got no money.'

'You already said.' Stevie glared at him.

'Is that a problem?' Dev asked.

'Well ... how can I...'

'Nick it, you fucking dickhead.'

'No.' Martin shook his head, amazed that

he'd said it.

It took all of three seconds for Dev to be at Martin's side and holding a knife under his nose.

'What?'

'I ... I daren't. I...'

'Get in there, get the booze, or go home to mummy dearest with half your fucking face falling off. And I'll be there to give her a matching cut.'

'OK ... OK.' Martin was so frightened, he could barely breathe. He quickly ran his tongue over his dry lips, as he kept repeating, 'OK ... OK.'

'That's better. Now go, 'Cause I'm real thirsty.'

'Cool, man.' Stevie winked at Dev.

'Yeah, and make sure they are cool.' Dev laughed. 'Do you get it, Fartin'?'

'Go on ... go on,' Stevie said, laughing as loud as Dev. 'Yeah, move it, Pissy Fartin',' Dev yelled.

Feeling sick to his stomach, trembling like a very old man, and with their taunts ringing loudly in his ears, Martin walked into the shop. This was the last thing he wanted to do. He hated himself for being so soft. Hated himself even more for what had happened last night. How could they do something so bad and laugh?

And what they had got up to this morning? They were keeping it close to their chest, whatever it was, just giving out snide remarks and in-jokes and laughing, laughing like the totally insane might laugh.

Quickly, he looked around in the dim light. At first he thought there was no one in the shop. There were two aisles, each laden with goods of all descriptions. He'd often heard the shopkeeper telling people that he had a bigger selection of soups than any supermarket. All anyone had to do was ask, and he would get in whatever their tiny heart desired.

Then, to his dismay, he spied a young girl of about nine years old talking to the shop-keeper, a small plump man with greying hair and moustache. Neither of them seemed to have realised that he'd come into the shop.

The booze was on the far side, stacked in packs of four. Slipping the hood of his red top up, he moved silently towards his target.

Get it. Get out. Get it. Get out. Round and round the mantra went in his head. Practically on the tips of his toes, he reached the stack of cans. Quickly, before he had a chance to think about it, he grabbed the top pack, shoved it under his top, and turned and ran.

Only the little girl was at the door and standing in his way.

CHAPTER NINETEEN

'What's happened? Claire asked, in a cloud of cigarette smoke as she dropped her cigarette into a small bin by the back door. Squeezing past Jill, she rushed over to her mother, her long, thick blonde hair tied loosely at the back of her neck with a pink band. She turned her blue eyes to Kerry.

'She fainted,' Kerry answered. Thinking, not again! What the hell is going on today?

First Doris, now her mother.

She pulled a face at Claire. Kerry hated the smell of cigarettes, and it seemed as if Claire was smoking more each day. She also hated Claire's breasts, because they were easily twice the size of her own.

Vanessa groaned and struggled to sit upright. 'Claire ... Claire, is that really you?' She reached out with her hand and touched her daughter's cheek. This one she'd nearly lost once. She could never go through it again.

'Well, yeah,' Claire answered. 'Who else would it be?'

'I thought ... I thought... Never mind.' Pushing everyone's hands away, Vanessa took a deep breath and stood up.

'I'm all right,' she said, as Sandra tried to

usher her into the front room.

'So you say, but just sit down a bit, yes?'

In the kitchen, Kerry backed Claire into the corner as Jill said, 'I ... er, I'll catch you later.' She made a hasty retreat back to her own house. She'd seen Kerry kick off before.

'Where the hell have you been?' Kerry demanded. 'And don't say school. You've been out all night, haven't you? That's why she fainted when Jill said about that girl being killed up Houghton Cut.'

'What girl?'

'Never fucking mind. Where have you been?'

Claire shrugged. 'Nowt to do with you, you're not me mother. So f–'

Before she could finish, Kerry slapped her, hard, leaving a red handprint on her cheek.

Claire gasped, her own hand rushing up to her stinging face. 'That hurt, you fucking bitch!'

'Yeah, and it'll hurt again.' Kerry lifted her hand, and Claire backed further away. 'Do you realise how hard she's trying? All she's been through, all we've all been through. Have you forgotten already? What if she gives up? It's a lifetime curse, you idiot, any-thing could tip her over the edge.'

Slowly Claire nodded. 'I'm sorry.' She burst into tears. 'Really, I'm sorry, it just seemed–'

'Like a good idea, yeah. Selfish bitch that

you are.'

Claire made her escape then, and ran for the stairs, but Kerry was hard on her heels and caught her at the bottom. Grabbing the sleeve of her coat, she spun her round. 'I'm warning you, pull a stunt like that again and boy, are you for it.'

'Let me go.' Claire yanked her arm back.

'Get up them stairs now before you feel my foot up your fucking arse, selfish cow.'

'What's going on out there?' Vanessa shouted.

Shaking her head, Claire ran up the stairs and into her room, slamming the door behind her as Kerry yelled from the bottom of the stairs, 'From now on, I'm watching you... And just wait till our Robbie gets in.'

This time, it was Sandra asking what was going on, as she came to the sitting room door.

'Nowt,' Kerry snapped, walking past Sandra and going in to her mother.

Pale faced, Vanessa sat back with her head resting on the back of the chair.

'You all right, Mam?'

Vanessa turned to her daughter. 'I was terrified, Kerry, when she didn't come home, but I didn't want to worry you or the others. And then when Jill said a young girl had been found dead up Houghton Cut ... I ... I thought it was her ... our Claire.'

She shook her head, then buried her face

104

in her hands and sobbed, all the pain and suffering she'd gone through rushing back to torment her.

Kerry was at her side in moments. She put her arms around her mother. 'God, our Claire is such a stupid, selfish cow. I could strangle her for putting you through this.'

Sandra said, 'I'll put the kettle on in a minute.' She moved over to Vanessa and rubbed her arm. 'Come on, love, it's all turned out right in the end. You know it has.'

'Mam, you've got to stop keeping these things in. You know what they said at the AA about stress, and bottling it up's not gonna help.'

Vanessa wiped her eyes. 'I know you're right, but ... but I've been such a selfish cow myself for years... Can you really blame our Claire?'

Sandra sighed. She didn't know what to say. She and Vanessa had been friends since infants school. The only break they'd had was when she had moved south for six years, and they had lost contact. She'd come home to find Vanessa the mother of five kids, and an alcoholic.

And yes, Vanessa had been selfish. The kids had gone without for the longest time. While most of the money was spent on booze, Sandra had despaired of her ever changing. But this last year she had been nothing short of fantastic, back to the old Vanessa, and a hint of the fantastic sense of humour she used to have showing through more and more. She kept to regular AA meetings, and there was always someone to go with her. Sandra shared the duty with Kerry and Robbie.

But something like this could fairly knock her off track, Sandra thought, but said, 'Look, I'm just gonna pop over and see if Jacko's back, find out about what's up with Doris, then I'll make us some tea, eh?'

Vanessa nodded gratefully.

Sandra was walking down Jacko's path when he pulled up in his ancient, beat up red car. Hearing the car come to a noisy stop, Sandra turned and, spotting Doris sitting grinning at her in the passenger seat, breathed a heavy sigh of relief and hurried back up the path.

'Oh, I'm so glad you're all right, Doris. For God's sake, you had me worried sick.'

'She had us all worried sick,' Mr Skillings said, pushing his door open and getting out of the back of the car.

Sandra nodded as she helped Doris to stand up, as Jacko came around the other side.

'I'm all right,' Doris insisted. But they took an arm each and helped her down the path, followed by Mr Skillings and his ever tapping cane.

When they had got her seated in the armchair beside the fireplace, Sandra said, 'So – what's the verdict, then?'

'Please, we ain't in court,' Doris replied.

'Now, Mam, no need for that. Sandra's only asking.'

'It's all right, Jacko.' Sandra smiled and turned to Doris. 'I know what the miserable so and so is like.'

Jacko laughed. 'Well, that's true.'

'I am here, you know.'

'Don't we just!' Jacko laughed again.

'Well? I'm waiting.' Sandra raised her eyebrows at Doris.

'I'm fine, they think when I fainted... Oh, that poor, poor girl.' Doris sighed as a picture in full blown Technicolor of what they had seen in the shop window entered her mind. 'They ... they think I must have banged my head and knocked myself out when I fainted, that's all. The heart's as strong as ever.'

'But I thought, with concussion, surely they should have kept you in?' Sandra glanced at Jacko, who shrugged and looked at his mother.

'She refused to stay,' Mr Skillings put in.

'That'll be right.' Sandra shook her head. 'What we gonna do with you, Doris?'

'I'm OK, and I don't want any fuss.'

The door opened, and Sally James from next door came in.

'You all right, chuck?' she asked.

'Yes, thank you, I'm fine, Sally. If only this

bloody lot would stop fussing.'

'Good. Just thought I'd let you know that the bairn came home about half an hour ago, something up at school with the heating, so her class got sent home. It's flaming cold, isn't it?'

'You're right there,' Mr Skillings said. 'Cold enough to freeze the balls off a brass monkey.'

Ignoring him, Sally went on, 'Anyhow, I gave her some coppers for the shop, but I thought you should know – because she's not back yet.'

CHAPTER TWENTY

Using the police car with an official driver and sirens blasting, Lorraine's thoughts were going as fast as the car as they made their way to Sunderland General Hospital.

What the hell happened?

She shook her head. How did he get so drunk that he didn't know where the hell he was?

Why would someone who barely drinks at all get in such a state?

A row with his partner?

Didn't happen!

I hardly think a disagreement over a few

flaming baubles would upset him enough for him to get that fucking drunk. That is definitely not Luke's way.

The landlord at the Beehive had said that Luke had been the last to leave the pub, and he thought that Luke had been in the toilets when his friends left.

I guess that's why the others thought he'd already gone home before them.

She grabbed hold of the car door as they took a rather tight corner, glancing quickly over at the young male driver. She gritted her teeth, but waited until they were back on all four wheels before asking, 'Just how fucking long have you been doing this?'

'First day on the job, ma'am.' He smiled proudly, showing extra large teeth with a huge gap in the middle as he looked at her in the rear view mirror.

'Eyes front,' she snapped. 'Especially if you want another day on the job.'

'Yes, ma'am.'

'And fucking well slow down.'

'Yes, ma'am.'

Just in time, he slowed down and avoided crashing into a blue minivan that had stopped at the lights, which had Lorraine shaking her head at him. A few minutes later, they were at the hospital.

Surprised that they had arrived in one piece, Lorraine jumped quickly out of the car. 'Wait,' she said. 'I don't know how long

I'm going to be. If it looks like an all day job, I'll phone you and send you back...' She shook her head. 'In fact, just go. I'll phone for a lift when I'm ready.'

'Yes, ma'am.'

She cringed. She hated being called ma'am, that's why her own squad called her 'boss'.

'What's your name, officer?'

'PC Jones, ma'am.'

'OK. I'll remember that, the next time I need a driver.'

'Thank you, ma'am.' He beamed from ear to ear.

Shaking her head, Lorraine hurried into the hospital. She flashed her ID at the receptionist, and asked for Luke's ward. After being given directions, she headed for the lift. Soon she was on the right floor, finding his room a few moments later, simply because there was a uniformed officer on guard outside of his door.

'Is this really needed?' she demanded.

'Orders, ma'am.'

'Whose orders?' she asked, although she already knew the answer.

'DI Fyfe's, ma'am.'

Gritting her teeth again, and telling herself to keep calm, she looked through the window into his room. She saw a doctor with a stethoscope on the left side of the bed, listening to Luke's chest, and a nurse on the other side of the bed taking his blood pressure.

'Jesus,' she muttered. For a few more minutes she stood and watched, her heart aching at the sight of Luke's battered face. 'OK – gotta ... got to go in.' Pulling her shoulders back, she entered the room. Although she walked with confidence, and a fixed smile on her face, she could not keep the shock from showing in her eyes.

The doctor spun round from the bed when he heard her. 'You know him? A relative, a friend, perhaps?'

'Yes, he ... he's my ... we live together. Please, what's wrong with him?'

'I would say he's been beaten up and left for dead. In this weather, I'm very surprised he's not. As it is, he's suffering from mild hypothermia, and I wouldn't be too surprised if pneumonia sets in. Don't be upset by the state his face is in. Nothing really to worry about there, it'll heal without leaving scars.'

'What?' Lorraine gasped, moving quickly to Luke's bed and taking hold of his hand.

'We are doing our best, trust me. We have his temperature under control, which is good, but–' He looked at her, gauging her reaction. Deciding that she looked strong enough to take the truth, he went on, 'The next twelve hours are critical. But now that you're here, it should help. Talk to him.'

Talk to him, she thought. Her heart pounding, she looked closely at the bruised and battered face of the man she loved, her mind focusing on what the doctor had not said about the next twelve hours.

Critical in what way?

'Please don't die, Luke,' she muttered when the doctor left. 'Please... I love you, Luke. Anyhow, the doctors always tell you the worst case, don't they, Luke? I know you'll get better.'

As she sat there staring at an unresponsive Luke, she tried to figure out why someone should do this.

Luke has no enemies.

Scratch that. All friggin' coppers have enemies, it comes with the job.

But who? And why?

Could be some mindless thug.

No... Gotta be someone he sent down.

Someone who's just got out, maybes.

How old of a case though? Months? Years? Or just some creep off the street fancying his chances?

She pulled her phone out. In a few moments, Sanderson answered. 'Yes, boss?'

'Find out who has recently been released from jail, that Luke arrested.'

'Boss!'

'Just do it, Sanderson, then let me know as soon as you can.'

'How far back?'

'As far as you can.'

'How is he?'

'Not good.'

'All right, but you know we can both get in trouble for this, especially if you know who finds out.'

'Who's gonna tell her?'

Sanderson sighed. 'OK, I'm on it.'

Switching her phone off, Lorraine looked at Luke.

Whoever the fuck has done this, God help them, she silently vowed.

Because I'm coming for you. And it won't be to talk.

CHAPTER TWENTY-ONE

'Get out the way, stupid kid,' Martin snarled at the girl.

Melanie Musgrove tried her best, but instead ended up doing a sort of awkward tap dance.

Martin, terrified in case he was going to get caught, pushed her just as he got the door open and she fell through. Falling on her knees, Melanie yelled out in pain. Martin tripped over her and the cans fell to the floor, landing in the middle of a dirty puddle of melted snow-water.

'Stupid fucking idiot,' Stevie shouted, as the shopkeeper came to the door to see what all the noise was about. He spotted the cans and guessed immediately what had happened. In a rage that someone should try to steal from him, when he had lived on the Seahills all his life and never once in all that time had any bother, he grabbed Martin's hood with one hand and reached for the cans with the other.

'Drop them,' Dev yelled, pulling his knife and yanking Melanie up by her hair. 'Or I'll fucking cut her. I will, so don't fucking tempt me.'

'No!' Melanie screamed. 'I want me dad, now. Dad!' She yelled as hard as she could. 'Get him off... Get him off.'

The shopkeeper froze. The last thing he wanted was to see Melanie hurt over a few cans of beer. He'd known her all her short life, and his wife was a friend of her grand-mother. And God help this bastard when Jacko found out.

'I want me dad.' She screamed again as loud as she could, struggling to be free. 'Mr Janson, get me dad, please, Mr Janson, I want me dad.'

Regaining his senses, the shopkeeper let go of Martin and defiantly dropped the cans back into the puddle.

'Clever twat,' Dev said, running the flat side of the blade across Melanie's cheek.

'No!' Martin yelled. 'Leave her alone. I'll get the cans. Don't hurt her.' Quickly, he snatched the cans out of the puddle. 'For fuck's sake, just let her go.'

Dev sneered at him, as he said to Stevie, 'Got a right soft shite here, haven't we? Gotta good mind to cut her just for the fun of it. Wanna see her bleed, Fartin'?'

'No ... I'll do anything, just don't hurt her.'

Dev paused for a moment, the blade hovering over Melanie's face as she stared at it in horrified fascination.

'Please don't... I mean it, I will do anything you say,' Martin said again.

'Anything?'

'Aye, whatever you want. Just don't hurt her.'

Worried because the shopkeeper knew him, and would definitely be calling the cops, Stevie tried to save his own skin while appearing to suck up to Dev. Because the last thing he really wanted was to see the kid hurt, there was no need.

Then he shrugged. What the fuck, I'm going soft.

He quickly reverted back to type, convincing himself that he was not too bothered about the kid. It was knowing that he would be banged straight up again as an accomplice that really bothered him. And he knew that Dev would do it on a whim. Dev was one fairly fucked up dude, and that was a fact.

'Thought you – we – had things to do.' He said out of the corner of his mouth to Dev.

'I have.'

'Well they're not gonna get fucking done if we're banged up again. Think about it.' Stevie was starting to feel a bit desperate. He thought last night had, on the whole, been an accident at first, but this fucker seemed hell bent on destroying anything or anyone who got in his way.

Dev thought about it and, with a snarl, pushed Melanie, who was now quietly sobbing for her father, away from him.

'Shut up, you little twat.'

Free now, Melanie jumped up out of the puddle she had fallen in and yelled a very defiant, 'No!'

Dev raised his fist and took a step towards her. 'Mouthy little git, aren't you?'

'You just wait till my dad gets you,' Melanie retorted, stepping back towards the shop.

The shopkeeper ran towards them. 'Leave her alone. Now. She's just a kid,' he yelled.

'Fuck you,' Stevie said, raising his fists and taking a very quick step towards the shopkeeper before turning and following Martin, and yelling at Dev to run.

Dev waved his knife at the shopkeeper. He so wanted to plunge it into his guts and twist. But Stevie was right, he had other things to do, and nothing could get in the way. Turning, he ran with the others, shouting over his shoulder, 'Call the cops and we'll be back, twat face. I mean it. This sink dump of a shop could do with a little warming. Brighten the place up, like.' He laughed as he kept on running.

'Bastards!' the shopkeeper yelled after them, as he helped Melanie into the shop.

'Me dad'll kill them, Mr Janson.'

'I know he will, pet. It's finding them first, though.'

'Me knees is really sore.'

'I'll get Mrs Janson down to bathe them. But ... Melanie, pet, I know you have to tell your dad what happened, but please don't tell Mrs Janson what that crazy one said about torching the place. I don't want her to worry. Just say you fell in the puddle, please. I'll have a word with your dad about it.'

'Are you not gonna tell the police, like?'

'I think it would be prudent not to.'

'What's prudent mean?'

Mr Janson chewed on his bottom lip and sighed. 'Safer, Melanie. It means safer.'

He went to the back stairs in the shop and shouted to his wife.

'What's up with you, hollering at the top of your voice like that? Anybody would think the place was on fire,' she said, coming down the stairs.

Mr Janson gestured with his head towards Melanie.

'What the...?' she said, taking one look at Melanie. 'Oh, you poor bairn.'

CHAPTER TWENTY-TWO

It was dark, so dark that he couldn't even see his hand as he held it in front of his face. Total blackout.

He was lying on his side, this much he knew. His right side and his leg hurt like hell.

His heart was banging against his ribs in fear.

Where am I? he thought, trying not to cry.

What happened?

Why am I here?

He could remember nothing.

Then an even more frightening thought entered his mind. Who am I?

He bit down on his lip to stop a scream.

'Who am I?' he slowly muttered as he tried hard to search for memories, but there was nothing there, not even a tiny glimmer for him to latch on to. No name, nothing. It was as if he wasn't even born, had never lived a life.

Something was trickling into his eye. He

guessed that it was blood. Lifting his hand to wipe it away, he felt a deep gash in his forehead where the blood was running quite quickly.

He gasped in fear and, gulping for air, tried to sit up. But the pain was so intense that he flopped back down again. 'Help me ... help me...' he whimpered. 'Please, somebody help me.'

It was then that he started screaming once, twice, into the dark. A moment later, he was unconscious.

CHAPTER TWENTY-THREE

Sanderson had ferreted out what he could on the case of the dead girl found on Houghton Cut, without letting DI Fyfe find out that he was looking. 'Apparently,' he said to Dinwall, over his egg and cress sandwich, 'her name is, or was, Tammy Dutsworth. She belongs in Hetton le Hole, and was walking home after a night out with her friends in Sunderland.'

'Wrong time, wrong place?'

'Apparently. She's ... was ... seventeen.'

'When are these kids ever gonna learn?'

'Probably never. A few drinks down their throats, and they all become invincible.

Most of us have been there.'

Dinwall took a bite of his own roast beef sandwich, chewed for a moment, then said, 'So, she have any enemies, or what?'

'Squeaky clean is the word. Didn't even have a boyfriend, so we can rule that out.'

'So basically we're looking for one nasty mad bastard.'

'Two. Don't forget our own case.'

'Huh, and that's firmly stuck in the mud. Seems from the girl in the card shop next door, who she became friendly with, this one did have a boyfriend. Only, the card shop girl never saw him, and the victim never once told her his name.'

'Weird.'

Sanderson put his crusts on the paper plate. Staring at them with a frown, Dinwall poked them with his finger. 'You should eat them, best part of the bread.'

'You eat them.'

'Very funny, ha ha. You'll be telling me to jump in the bowl next, like one of those chocolate sweets.'

'I wish.'

The phone rang, and Dinwall snatched it up just before Sanderson's outstretched hand reached it. 'Hi, boss, how is he?'

After a moment, he shook his head at Sanderson and mouthed, No change.

'Shit,' Sanderson said quietly.

'OK, boss.' He handed the phone to

Sanderson, 'She wants to speak to you.'

Taking the phone, Sanderson put it to his ear. Dinwall tried to keep up with the many nods Sanderson gave, but after nine he gave up and stared out of the window.

'Ever been to Galashiels?' Sanderson asked, when he put the phone down.

'That'll be a big fat no... Er, why?'

''Cause you're about to visit it. I'll pick you up in a half an hour. Gotta pop home for something.'

'What, Galashiels? That's in flaming Scotland ain't it? So how long does it take to get there?'

'An hour and three quarters, give or take a few minutes.'

Dinwall stood up and headed for the door, muttering under his breath. 'Not with you driving, mate. Be lucky if we get there next week.'

'I heard that!'

CHAPTER TWENTY-FOUR

The door to the Blue Lion was wedged wide open, in a welcoming sort of way, though people didn't seem to be taking the offer up as they passed the doors quite quickly. Martin followed Stevie and Dev into the pub, passing below the Under New Management sign.

Martin hadn't said a word all the way up to Houghton from the shop on the corner of the Seahills. Instead, he'd spent the time thinking, trying as hard as he could to work out a way to get away from them without them hurting his mother, because the way things were going, it could only get worse. He had also noticed that since Dev had taken the piss out of the way Stevie swaggered about the place, Stevie had adopted a more sedate style, and kept his hands mostly in his pocket now. If these two were to fall out, then that would make things easier – but how to make that happen?

He had come to the conclusion that if Stevie Masterton was frightened of Dev, then he himself should be more than frightened. And he was. He felt as if his very brain was shaking, alongside every part of his body. How he wished he'd never got involved with Stevie Masterton.

What had happened last night had been horrendous, and really terrified the life out of him. He knew that things would only get worse. He sighed, Dev seemed determined to take revenge for something that had happened a long time ago, and had nothing to do with the people he was taking it out on, already today was turning into a nightmare.

He had made an excuse to go home after what had happened last night. His whole body had not been able to stop shaking. Though the first hit had been shocking, it had been what happened next. He had no words to explain what he had felt, he'd only known that he'd had to get away. Dev had invited himself to stay at Stevie's house, and this morning Martin had been hoping – no, praying – they wouldn't come calling for him.

Perhaps forget he even existed.

But no such luck.

He sighed. Would he ever be free?

The face of the woman behind the bar was in shadow, but there was something about her that Martin recognised. He couldn't quite place her, he guessed that Stevie had too, by the way he suddenly stopped dead in his tracks.

Then Martin realised just who the woman was.

Oh, God, no! Not her.

He wanted to run. The urge was so strong that his legs shook. He desperately needed to be anywhere but here.

Why hadn't he had the guts to tell them last night to just fuck off and leave him alone?

'Well, hello, boys.'

Martin stared at her face. Yes, it's her. The face is different... She must have had something done.

That's it, that plastic surgery thing. Her lips are like a pair of fat fucking slugs. God, she's worse than she was. She ... she actually looks plastic.

But that voice of hers... Unforgettable. Reminds me of someone scraping glass down me back.

He shivered, and looked quickly around for an escape route. But as usual for him, there was none. The door had mysteriously closed behind them.

Then he saw Jason Smith in the shadows.

'You!' Stevie said, staring at the woman in front of them.

'Yes, it is I. And who are you?' She turned her face from Stevie to Dev.

If the other two were intimidated, then Dev certainly was not. 'The name's Dev, and that's all you'll ever need to know.' He curled his lip at her.

She leaned over the bar and locked eyes with him. 'I suggest you come back in ten minutes, after you've had a small talk with your friends here. Let them out!' she suddenly yelled at Jason Smith.

Jason hurried to the door.

'You!' she yelled again. They all turned to look at her. Raising her hand, she pointed her finger at Stevie, turned her hand upside down and beckoned with her finger. 'Here, now.'

It took him only a few seconds to cross the space between them. When he reached the bar, she grabbed the front of his top and, thrusting her face in his, and said, 'Get him in order boy, or it won't only be him that suffers. Got it?'

Staring at her, Stevie slowly nodded. She let go of him and, with a toss of her head, dismissed him, only to shout, 'Ten minutes, brat. That's all you've got.'

Outside, Martin was leaning up against the wall with Dev's elbow at his throat. When he heard Stevie, Dev let go of Martin and snarled, 'Who the fuck does she think she fucking well is? The bastard's lucky I didn't tear the place apart.'

Stevie shook his head. 'No way... That's the last thing you want to be doing.'

'Look here.' Dev towered threateningly over Stevie. 'You promised me some easy money till I've finished what has to be done here. What the fuck is going on?'

'She's it.'

'What the fuck?'

'The money. All we have to do is sell for her, piece of piss, only...'

'Only what, for fuck's sake?'

'She's the boss mate. Screw with her, and we're all fucking dead.'

'A woman!'

'Yeah, well, she isn't just any woman. I didn't even know when I got the fucking message that it was from her, else even I would have kept out of her way. Trust me she's way, way out of our league.'

'There's no woman alive can put the fucking frighteners on me, mate.' He raised his fist to punch Stevie. 'Just who the fuck do you think you're talking too.'

'He's right,' Martin mumbled. Even though he would love to see Stevie get his just desserts, time was moving on. If she had to come looking, then God help them all.

'What'd you say?' Dev dropped his fist.

Martin looked away not wanting to face Dev, but knowing that yet again he had no choice he slowly moved his gaze from Dev's feet to his face. 'She's evil... Pure evil.'

'Sounds like my kind of woman.' Dev nodded his head. 'What we waiting for, then?'

They turned back and, judging by the smug look on his face, Dev really had no idea who the woman behind the bar was.

CHAPTER TWENTY-FIVE

Jacko decided to give Melanie ten more minutes before he went looking for her, but five minutes later he was pacing the floor and looking out the window.

'Just go and look for her, son, I'll be all right.'

'But...'

'No buts. Go and find the bairn, 'cause you won't settle until she's back. But I'm betting she'll be playing on the swings in the park with her friends.'

'I'll go and get Mr Skillings to sit with you.'

'Don't you dare. The last thing I need is a baby sitter, and if I hear his flaming cane tap once more this day, I swear I won't be responsible for my actions. So, now, get yourself away.'

'Right, but I'll not be long.'

At the gate, Jacko looked up the street, then swung his head in the other direction. He decided to go to the swing park first, because there had certainly been enough time for her to get to the shop and back.

The park was behind Daffodil Terrace. As he walked through the cut between number seven and eight, he could see a bunch of kids playing on the swings, and recognized them as a couple of Melanie's friends. Smiling, he walked over to Emma Lumsdon.

'Hi, Emma. Have you seen our Melanie?'

She stopped the swing with her feet. 'Not since she said she was going to the shop, ages ago. She said she was coming here... But she hasn't.'

'Hmm.'

'Is she lost?'

'No, Emma, don't worry. She must be still at the shop.'

'But that was ages ago.'

'So you said.'

Jacko felt the hackles start to rise on the back of his neck, along with a feeling of dread that started in the pit of his stomach and rose slowly upwards.

Where is she? he thought, turning quickly and heading back in the direction of the shop, with a frowning Emma staring at his back. It took him all of three minutes to reach the shop, and he walked in to find Melanie perched on a stool with Mrs Jansen dabbing at her knees with a sponge.

Before he could reach her, Mr Jansen hurried from behind the counter and ushered a frowning Jacko outside. He quickly explained everything that had happened.

When he was finished, for a brief moment Jacko just stood there, his face going from red to purple as rage blinded him. Mr Janson thought he was going to have a heart attack, or at the very least some sort of fit. He put his hand on Jacko's shoulder.

Emotions raged through Jacko's body and mind. Someone had dared to hurt his Melanie.

Held a knife to his little girl's face and threatened her.

Kill, kill, was the uppermost thought in his

mind. He pictured his hands around the neck of the perpetrator, and squeezed as hard as he could. Squeezed the life out of the bastard.

But no. Slowly, common sense took over, calming the rage inside of him. Death was too good for the bastard!

Jacko took a deep breath and looked into Mr Janson's eyes, as his colour slowly returned to normal. Still expecting an explosion, Mr Janson dropped his hand and stepped back.

But Jacko was calm, as he said, in a cold, matter of fact voice that chilled Mr Janson far more than Dev had, 'I'll make the bastard suffer.'

'Twats is what they are, the three of them. Nowt but scum. They want locking up and the keys thrown away.' Mr Jenson said.

'But they're not gonna get locked up, are they? 'Cause you're not calling the cops.'

'He threatened to torch the place, Jacko.'

'And you believed him?'

'You didn't see him. The dirty bastard scumbag looked capable of anything... Er, I should say that Martin Raynor did try to sort of stop him.'

'Sort of?'

'He yelled at him to stop, and then promised to do anything he wanted if he didn't cut little Melanie.'

Jacko couldn't stop the shiver that coursed

through his body at the thought of Melanie being cut. The very word went straight to his core. He slashed at the air in front of him with his fist. 'Bastard bastard bastard.' He spun round his feet pounding the ground, he glared at the empty street.

'I swear to God I'll get the bastards.' He muttered. 'Nobody hurts my Melanie.'

Behind him Mr Janson prayed that no one would walk by. Especially if they looked and dressed like that nasty trio.

After a moment, Jacko said, 'Anything he wanted, eh?'

'Yes. Don't know what he meant by that, though. He looked terrified an'all.'

Jacko turned back round, and said. 'Martin wasn't too bad of a kid till a year or two ago. Got in with the flaming wrong one when he threw in with that Stevie Masterton, all right.'

Mr Janson nodded. He also remembered Stevie as once being a canny kid, though as he'd grown older he'd sharp fallen into the same ways as his bullying father and brothers. He also wondered just what Jacko was going to do. He knew Jacko well, and him being this quiet was not a good sign, not where Melanie was concerned. All he could think, even though he was in fear of them himself was, God help them, they picked on the wrong kid this time alright.

Jacko heaved a large sigh. After a

moment's thought, he said calmly, 'OK, Mr Janson. I won't say anything to your wife, but I think it's time I took Melanie home now. Thank you for looking after her.'

Silently, his fists clenched tightly in the pockets of his leather jacket, Jacko walked ahead of Mr Janson into the shop. There was no sign of Mrs Janson. Jacko could understand Mr Janson wanting to protect his wife and his livelihood, that was only natural, but his own priority was Melanie.

She was sitting on the stool, staring at the door, a worried frown on her face. When she saw him, the tears flowed freely down her face. Jacko felt as if his heart would burst. He picked his daughter up from the stool and held her close.

Melanie started to cry. Knuckling the tears out of her eyes, she whispered, 'They frightened me, dad. They were horrible.'

'I know, Melanie. Hush now. I'm here. It'll be all right. They won't ever touch you again.'

Swinging her round until she was on his back with her hands clasped around his neck, he looked down at her knees, and felt the flame of anger burning bright.

When I'm finished with the bastards, they'll be in no fit state to touch anyone ever again.

CHAPTER TWENTY-SIX

After making sure that Doris was all right, and sharing tea with Vanessa and her kids – where the talk soon turned to Darren, and the excitement started to build for a few hours time when they would all be at the game to cheer him on – Sandra went home.

She opened the door to her empty house, her immaculate, freshly painted, empty house. The hallway had cream walls with mahogany doors and skirting boards, and the light fittings on the walls, all four of them, were matching with tulip head globes. It was the same theme throughout the house. She'd seen it in one of her country house magazines, and wanted it so much. She had saved and saved, but it had been worth every penny. She flicked the sitting room lights on for a moment as she went and opened the curtains, because she'd forgotten to open them this morning, they had left so early. Then she collapsed on the brown leather settee and burst into tears.

Her nest was empty and, although immensely proud of all four sons, she was lonely like she had never been in her life. It had never bothered her that her husband

132

worked away most of the week, she'd always had the boys. But the change had come quickly, and her second son had left in September to join his brother at uni in London. The two younger boys, still in college, were visiting them for the week, kicking their heels in London and tasting freedom until they all came back up home together on Christmas Eve.

She slipped her shoes off, then ran her feet through the fur rug, and sighed as she dashed the tears from her face. A moment later, she jumped at the sudden loud knock on the door.

'Who the hell...?' she muttered. Around these parts, family and friends didn't knock, they opened the door and announced their presence, mostly by shouting, 'Anybody in?' A knock meant a stranger. Frowning, she slipped her shoes back on, and headed for the door.

The last person she expected to be there when she opened it was Stevie Masterton.

What the hell?

He grinned at her. Before she could voice her thoughts, he beat her to it by saying, 'I'm your new debt collector ... well, me and me friends are.'

Sandra's heart froze. For the first time since she had been married, she had been forced to go to a moneylender last year, despite all the times she'd chastised Doris and others, and helped them out when they were desperate. She'd been only too pleased that her circumstances were such that she'd never once had to go near a moneylender.

But now her husband's wages were not keeping up with inflation, and had not been for a number of years. She'd got the name of the lender from Doris, even though she'd harangued Doris for years not to use him. It hadn't been easy, but when she'd begged, Doris had given in, but pleaded with her to find another way.

There had not been any other way. Times changed. She'd even looked for a job, but there were none to be had. So far, with a struggle, she'd managed to keep payments up, and the debt a secret from her husband.

'What?' she gasped. 'How?'

'Just pay up.'

'But it's not due until the end of the month.'

'Sez you... Only the debt's been bought, see, and the new boss wants it today.'

'But I can't... I haven't got it.'

Sandra's face was chalk white, and she gulped hard when the young man in front of her changed his grin to a scowl.

'Well, I'll just have to take it then, won't I? Let's see what you've got.' He put one foot through the doorway, and raised his arm to push Sandra to one side.

Only Sandra was made of sterner stuff

than he'd first thought. Lifting her leg, she pulled it back, then kicked his shin as hard as she could. He let out a high pitched scream, as he reached for her throat with both hands. He should have remembered she was a fire cracker.

'Fuck off!' she yelled, slamming the door in his face. Quickly, she turned the key. Then, leaning against the wall, she took three or four deep breaths before looking out the window. She gasped. Another two, who she had not noticed at first, were walking down the path to her front door.

CHAPTER TWENTY-SEVEN

Lorraine held onto Luke's hand. His breathing was shallow. The doctors had told her that he was very poorly, and probably the only reason he wasn't actually fighting for his life was because he was exceptionally fit. 'Twelve hours outdoors in freezing temperatures. Not good,' the doctor had said, shaking his head at her, as if she was somehow to blame. And then he dropped the bombshell that it still could go either way.

'In other words, he knows fuck all. Don't die, Luke, please don't leave me,' she pleaded, tears running down her face.

But there was no answer from Luke. The man she loved might have been on another planet for all the notice he was taking. His eyes were tightly closed, his face was unmoving. She felt as if she was talking to herself.

'The doc says I have to talk to you, so you just better be listening, mister.' She wiped her eyes and sighed. 'I love you, Luke Daniels, so fucking well wake up and stop pissing about.'

'How is he?' A deep voice from behind startled her.

She turned to see Sanderson standing in the doorway. He was holding a bagful of green grapes, Luke's favourite fruit.

If only he was in a fit state to eat them, Lorraine thought, dashing another tear from her cheek.

Oh God, no, Sanderson thought, stepping quickly into the room. Reaching Lorraine, he put a comforting hand on her shoulder, then blew air out of his cheeks in relief when he saw that Luke was not dead. For a moment, from the stillness of the room and Lorraine's pale face, he'd feared the worst.

Lorraine's next words, though, froze him. 'He might die, Sandy. He still might die. Because to tell you the truth I don't think they have a fucking clue what's wrong with him.'

Sanderson took a deep breath. 'He won't die, Lorraine. He's tough as nails, is Luke.

Doctors always prepare you for the worst. Just hang in there... How many times have we seen victims at death's door, only for them to be up and walking the next day?'

Is that what Luke is, a victim? she thought, looking sadly at Sanderson.

'Oh, and I've phoned Mavis. I thought you might not have had time to get around to it. She's probably on her way now, with that crazy godmother of yours.'

'Thanks, Sandy. I did ring a couple of times, but there was no answer, again. God knows where she's been. A farmers market isn't that bloody interesting."

He squeezed her shoulder. 'Want something to drink?'

'Please, the usual.' Throughout the conversation, Lorraine had barely taken her eyes off Luke's face. For a brief moment, her heart fluttered. Had his eyelids moved? Next moment, she sighed as her heart once again plummeted. 'Just wishful thinking,' she muttered.

'Sorry?'

'Nothing.' She shook her head.

'OK. Can of Diet Coke coming up.' Sanderson hurried out of the room.

'Oh, my dear God,' Mavis said a minute later, hurrying over to the side of Luke's bed.

Lorraine gave her mother a small smile. Mavis was dressed in her usual hippy mode

– long blue cotton skirt with green swirls on it, long, heavy blue cardigan over a cream blouse, her fair hair tied up at the sides and flowing down her back. She missed the smile, as she was intent on looking at Luke.

She turned to her daughter. 'I'm sorry, something wrong with the phone it keeps switching itself off. So, what have they said?'

'Time. Rest.' Lorraine rubbed the back of Luke's hand. 'Talk to him...To tell the truth, Mam, they just haven't got a fucking clue.' Lorraine dropped Luke's hand, and buried her face in her own hands.

Mavis quickly moved round the bed just as her friend, Lorraine's godmother Peggy, walked in.

'So what's up then?' Peggy said. 'I just got your message.' She held her mobile up. Then she glanced at Luke. 'Oh, my God, the poor bairn.' Peggy, dressed in tight black leather jeans and black leather jacket, moved quickly to the bed.

Lorraine's lips twitched slightly when she heard Luke referred to as a poor bairn, and Mavis shook her head. Peggy was so melodramatic, even at the best of times.

'He's gonna be all right, isn't he?' She covered her cheeks with the palms of her hands, and turned to Lorraine. 'I so can't stand the smell of these places... Hope you're gonna catch the bastard who done this. Luke's a bloody good man, and he doesn't deserve this. 'Cause it's your job you know... You are supposed to be a copper.'

Just as Lorraine was about to explode all over Peggy, Sanderson walked in. 'We'll catch him, don't worry,' he said carrying three coffees and a can of Diet Coke on a tray. 'Saw you getting out of the lift, Mavis. And I guessed you wouldn't be far behind, Peggy.'

'Oh, just what I need, you lovely, lovely man,' Peggy said, flashing her eyes at Sanderson as she reached for a cup.

Blushing a violent shade of red, Sanderson handed the other drinks around. Mavis and Lorraine thanked him, as Lorraine flicked the ring pull on her can and it opened with a loud hiss.

A few minutes later, Sanderson made his excuses to go. Time to pick Dinwall up and head to Galashiels. There was just so much of Peggy he could take. He knew – well, he hoped – she was only joking, but for definite his wife wouldn't see it like that. She didn't like Peggy. She never had, although she'd never said anything bad about Mavis, and he guessed she quite liked Lorraine in her own way. Sanderson suspected that his wife didn't really like anybody else at all.

CHAPTER TWENTY-EIGHT

Jacko was finally satisfied that his mother would be all right, with Mr Skillings promising to look after her and Melanie. Although his mother had insisted they would certainly be all right on their own, Jacko felt that, after what had happened at the shop, and with those crazy bastards on the loose, there was safety in numbers.

Warning Melanie not to say anything to anybody about what had happened, least of all her grandmother, because Doris would hunt the bastards down herself, he had decided to bide his time. They would get what was coming to them, but on his terms, and when they least expected it.

Because he had to be doing something to keep his mind off it, and to stop him from looking for them right now and killing them with his bare hands, he thought that now would be as good a time as any to pop round to see Danny Jordan and the guys and find out more about Danny's latest crazy caper.

As he drove along the street, he spotted three ... men? boys? Sometimes it was hard to tell. Druggies, alkies, all seemed to lose all sense of time. In their thirties, they still dressed as teenagers, with their hoodies on. A couple of these looked vaguely familiar. He drove past, then recognised one of them. Stevie Masterton. His fingers tightened around the steering wheel until the veins stood out on his hands. He knew, if he confronted them now, he would kill the bastards, but that would be no good for his daughter or his mother. No. He had to stay calm, whatever it cost. He would get them, and boy, would they suffer. At least they were heading in the opposite direction to his house.

'What the hell is that prick Masterton doing back on the streets, anyhow?' he muttered. 'Thought the fucking toe-rag was banged up?'

He frowned, watching them through his rear view mirror. Had they just gone down Sandra Gilbride's path, or was it the angle of the car making it look like they had? He shrugged. Can't think of any reason why they would bother Sandra. Must be the curve in the road, as they walked through the alleyway. Sandra's a match for them twats, any day. But I think I'll pop in on my way back, just to make sure everything's all right. She is on her own at the moment, and the bastard has a knife.

He reached Danny's house, and pulled up behind Danny's beloved van, which he called Elizabeth, after his idol, Elizabeth Taylor. His wife went absolutely crazy whenever she heard him. You could always tell when he'd slipped up, first stop on their way home was a florists.

Jacko went up the path to find the front door slightly open, and on pushing it wide, he heard laughter coming from the kitchen. Closing the door behind him, he walked down the hallway and opened the kitchen door to find Len Jordan dressed as a very miserable looking Santa Claus, and Danny and Adam Glazier laughing their heads off.

Adam was as fair as the cousins were dark, tall, slim and, at twenty-seven years old, the youngest by far of the group. He was fast losing his hair, and hated any mention of the fact.

It didn't take long for gossip to spread on the Seahills and all three immediately asked how Doris was. When Jacko assured them that she was fine, Danny and Adam turned back to Len and burst out laughing again.

'Well, let's see what youse lot look like, then.' Len pulled a face at Jacko, as he picked a Santa suit up and threw it at Adam. 'Clever shits, they think the pair of them are gonna be heart-throb Santas.'

Jacko laughed knowing that Len was probably right. For a brief time, it relieved the tension he was feeling.

'Huh. You an' all?' Len curled his lip at Jacko.

Shaking his head, Jacko picked one of the

suits up from the kitchen bench. 'This one mine?'

'Aye, they're all large,' Danny replied, stripping his shirt and jeans off before reaching for the remaining suit.

As he was putting the pants on, Len looked at him. His eyes opened wide when he spotted Adam's bright lemon underpants with a cartoon character on each leg. 'Ugh,' Len said, looking the other way. He didn't realise a moment later, when the others burst out laughing, that he was the one they were laughing at.

When they were all dressed, white hair and beards firmly in place, Adam said, 'Shame to miss out, seeing as we're all dressed up. Why don't we pop over to the Metro Centre for an hour or so, bit of practice, like?'

'It'll take us ages to get to the Metro Centre this time of year,' Len said. 'I was stuck trying to get past it last week for nearly two hours. Daft bloody planners, doing a two lane road past the biggest shopping centre in Europe. They should have known better.'

'Hmm,' Danny said. 'You might have a point there.'

'I haven't got two hours to spare today, anyhow.' Jacko shook his head. 'How about the Broadway in Houghton? I can't be away no more than an hour.'

They mulled it over, but not for long, because a few minutes later four Santas were climbing into Danny's van. They reached the Broadway in less than five minutes. Danny dropped the lads off outside of the church, and parked the van at the far side next to the new block of flats (that was once a night club, and before that a factory) and in front of the pizza shop. Picking his collecting tin up off the passenger side floor, he headed back to his friends, smiling as he saw they were already at work.

Mentally he rubbed his hands together, imagining he could hear the sound of coins dropping into the tins. Clink clink magic. Yes!

He reached them and nodded at Adam, as a little old lady in a blue coat, with matching hat, put a pound coin in the tin and, smiling, wished Adam a merry Christmas as she walked away.

'See, what did I say? Everybody's gonna be happy, 'cause people feel good when they think they're helping others. See, the proof's in the pudding.'

'Thinking being the operative word,' Len said, with his usual scowl.

'Careful, cuz, you'll frighten the kiddies away with that face.'

Adam burst out laughing. 'Doesn't he anyhow?'

'Get stuffed.' Len glared at him, just stopping himself from calling Adam 'Yellow Knickers'.

'I've just got one thing to ask you, Len. You know when you look in the mirror on a morning? Does your reflection look the other fucking way?'

They all burst out laughing. Even Jacko couldn't help himself, especially watching the penny slowly drop. Len growled, 'Very funny.'

'OK, OK, enough,' Danny said, trying hard to wipe the grin off his face. 'We can't be arguing here. Now, come on, get to work.' He walked up to a smiling couple with a toddler in a pushchair. The woman was about to open her purse when the little girl spotted Danny and started screaming. Quickly, the woman threw an apologetic smile as they walked away.

'Hah! Who's frightening the kids now?' Len smirked.

Fuck off, Danny mouthed at him, then turned to a six year old boy who eagerly put fifty pence in his tin.

'Can I have a new bike?' he demanded, his skinny arms folded across his chest.

'With that attitude, you can have anything you like, son.'

'What's att ... atti-tude?'

'Just another name for a blue bike.'

'I want a red one.'

'OK, OK, you can have any colour you want. No problemo!' Danny pulled a face at the others, who were trying hard not to laugh out loud.

'I don't think you're the real Santa, 'cause there's lots of you.' He looked at the other three. 'See, six of you.'

'The kid's seeing double. Gimme some of what he's on,' Adam blurted out, much to the amusement of his friends and people passing by.

'Why don't you go find your Mam, there's a good boy,' Danny said, trying hard not to grit his teeth.

'She's not lost.' The little boy looked at him with wide eyed innocence.

'Clever little shit,' Danny muttered under his breath.

Just then a dark haired young woman, in jeans and a white t-shirt, even though it was very cold, hurried up to him. 'Come here, Jake, what's the man been saying to you?' She frowned at Danny as if he'd done something wrong as she pulled her son towards her.

'Me? I haven't said anything!'

'So what's he frightened for?'

'Frightened?' Danny couldn't believe what he was hearing. 'He ... he's not. Far from it, actually.'

Len, Jack and Adam looked at each other, then quickly back at the mother. Len was just about to speak up in Danny's defence when the little boy burst into tears.

'See what I mean!' his mother shouted.

'But ... but...' Danny said.

'No buts. mister, I'm calling the cops. You're a fucking creep.' She swept her arm around to include them all. 'You're all a bunch of fucking creeps, probably one of them dirty bastard paedophile rings you hear about all the time.'

'But...' That was as far as Danny got.

Jacko moved forward. 'There's no need for that. Don't you think you're overreacting a bit?'

'Yeah, quite a bit, an' all,' a voice behind him said. Jacko turned to see a young girl, who he recognised as the oldest of Len's two daughters, Carol.

Carol had inherited her father's height, but that was all. Her looks were purely her mother's. Her hair was dyed the blackest of black, and her face was made up Goth style.

On seeing Carol, who towered above her, the boy's mother, still clutching his arm, stepped back. 'I ... er... I don't want no trouble, Carol.'

'Should have thought about that before you accused my uncle of being a nonce, then, shouldn't you? And just let me grab your arm the way you've got hold of the kid's, just maybes you might cry, eh?'

'I might have been a bit too hasty.' Her mouth trembled.

'A bit!'

'Why ... em ... we better go, son.'

'Not so fucking quick.'

Len, who had, a moment ago, been proud of his daughter for saving the day, frowned at her.

'You have something to say to my uncle before I call the police. 'Cause I know you've pulled this scam more than once, you nasty horrible cow.'

'What?' Danny, full of indignation now, practically yelled in the woman's face.

She looked at Danny, guilt and fear in her eyes, dropping her head she took off at a run, dragging the boy, who was still crying, behind her. Glaring at her retreating figure, Carol pulled her mobile out.

'Er, no, love.' Danny put his hand over her phone. 'Best not.'

Carol looked at her father, and Len cringed. She swung her head back to her uncle. 'But she's been getting away with this for God knows how friggin' long.'

Len cringed again.

'I think it's time we called it a day,' Jacko said with finality. Not willing to argue about it, he turned round and headed back to the van. With a shrug, Adam followed.

Len looked from his daughter to his cousin. Reaching out, he patted his daughter's arm. 'Thanks, pet.'

'Yeah. Thanks from me, an' all.' Danny smiled at his niece and patted her other arm.

'OK, guys, I'm not a dog. Tell me, please –

148

just when are youse lot gonna grow up?' She shook her head, but smiled as she walked away.

Back at the van, Jacko and Adam were standing at the door. They watched as their two friends walked towards them.

'You reckon the Metro Centre's off, then?'

Jacko shrugged. 'We don't want a repeat performance like that again, do we?'

'That's for sure.' Adam nodded. 'Once you get branded a fucking nonce, your life might as well be over, 'cause there's always some that'll believe the bastard worst, even if you're innocent.'

Reaching them, Danny opened the door. 'Friggin' hell, do you think anybody will know that was me? 'Cause there was a few people knocking around,' he asked, when they were all in the van and sitting down.

Adam glanced at Jacko, and pulled a face. 'Why, not likely, man.'

'But our Carol knew it was me.'

'That's because she's your niece, thicko, she knows you.'

'So does half of fucking Houghton!'

Shaking his head, Danny started the engine.

'Guess that's this idea knocked on the head then,' Jacko said.

For a brief moment the others were quiet, then they all nodded their heads in agreement. 'Yeah, really couldn't go through that again,' Danny said, pulling up outside his house.

Adam shook his collecting tin. 'We gonna count what's in these?'

'Aye, why not. Might be enough for a pint each,' Len said, opening the top of his tin and looking inside. 'It's been a long day, and I'm thirsty.'

'Wow!' he said, a moment later. 'Somebody's popped a fiver in here.' He tipped the contents onto the seat, and quickly the others did the same.

'Fucking hell,' Adam yelled, a few minutes later. 'Twenty-nine quid.'

'I've got eighteen,' Jacko said.

'Twenty-two here,' Danny said, grinning at them.

They all turned to Len, who was still counting.

'Come on.' Adam poked Len's arm.

'Shut up. I'll forget where I was.'

Adam sighed and shook his head, while the others grinned. Finally, a triumphant Len said, 'Thirty-four quid.'

'That makes it...' Adam said.

'One hundred and three quid!' Danny shouted. 'Who's for the Metro Centre?'

Jacko sighed. He'd never been keen on this idea in the first place, and what had happened today had reaffirmed his worst fears. But that amount of easy money...

The others had already shouted their

agreement, and were now looking expect-
antly at Jacko. He hesitated, still not happy.
Finally he said, 'OK ... OK. But the first
sign of any carry-on like today's and I'm
outta there, pronto.'

After much back slapping from the others,
and his cut of the money in his pocket,
Jacko headed home.

CHAPTER TWENTY-NINE

He blinked slowly, then his eyes were open.
But again there was only blackness.

Scared, he bit his lip and tasted blood.

Am I blind?

Who am I?

He had no recollection of having already
woken up once. All he could feel was pain.

He missed no one, because there was no
one to miss.

No one to cry out to.

All alone.

In the dark.

CHAPTER THIRTY

Having Emma home, because of the heating breaking down in her classroom, blew Vanessa's plans. Christmas shopping with Emma was not a good idea. Unlike other little girls, Emma hated shopping of any kind. Plus, she had a mouth on her as big as Tynemouth, and Vanessa knew she would spot the tiniest item for one of the others that she tried to hide from her. Claire was sulking upstairs, and it would be pointless to ask her to baby-sit as she and Emma did not get on at all.

She sighed. This would be the first Christmas in a long time that Vanessa could remember being sober. Last year had been hard, and went by in a blur, because all she could think about was wanting a drink. And another!

'But I'm over it now, and I so want to make this year extra special.'

She picked up Darren's blue t-shirt and spread it out on the ironing board, then snatched it up and breathed in the smell of him and sighed. She was so proud. They would all be there tonight to cheer him on, the whole family. She knew Robbie especially couldn't wait.

She put the t-shirt back on the ironing board and ran the iron over it, remembering when she'd first tackled the family ironing. Robbie had gasped with delight, and hugged her.

That small gesture had brought it home just how much pressure Robbie and Kerry had been under, and just what she had put her family through, day after day. She'd felt both humble and ashamed. All those years wasted.

But it was over now. She wasn't just on the mend, because she wasn't broken any more.

Without thinking about it, and as if it was the most natural thing in the world, Vanessa started to sing as she got on with the rest of her ironing.

Upstairs, Claire heard her, and quietly came to the top of the stairs, where she stood in wonder. She'd forgotten, and guessed they all had, just what a beautiful voice their mother had.

She sat down on the top stair and cried as her mother went through half a dozen songs, from *Stand By Me* to *Bridge Over Troubled Water*.

When Vanessa fell quiet, Claire dried her eyes and went downstairs.

'Want a cuppa, Mam?'

'That would be nice, Claire. And one of our Robbie's mates dropped a bag full of goodies off – sure there's some of those chocolate biscuits you love.'

Claire smiled at her mother as she moved towards the gas cooker. Our Kerry's right. I am a selfish bitch. Mam is trying so hard, she thought, as she filled the kettle up and put it on the gas ring. I shouldn't have stayed out last night. With a sigh, she turned to Vanessa. 'Mam, I'm sorry. Really I am.'

Vanessa put the iron down and opened her arms. 'It's all right, pet. Come here.'

Claire quickly entered the comforting circle of her mother's arms. She had missed this so much over the past years. She never wanted to risk losing it again. She sniffed, and noticed that there was no smell of stale alcohol, which had been part of her mother for as long as she remembered. Instead, she smelled a familiar perfume.

Lifting her head up to look at Vanessa, she said, 'You've been nicking my new scent, haven't you?'

Vanessa grinned. 'Sorry, love, but it's gorgeous.'

'I thought it was going down fast. I was gonna blame our Kerry, even though I never smelled it on her.'

'Well, I'm pleased that disaster's been averted.'

Stepping back, Claire smiled. 'You get the biscuits, Mam, and I'll do the tea.'

A few minutes later, they were sitting watching the news on the television. Much was being said about the two murders in one night at Houghton le Spring. As usual, the newsreader pronounced Houghton wrong, and Vanessa tutted.

She looked at Claire as he went on about the young girl in Houghton Cut. There was still no news on who the girl was, and Vanessa couldn't help but say, 'I so pity her parents.'

'What about the girl?'

'Of course, her an' all. Poor soul... Claire?'

Claire sighed. 'Sorry, Mam.'

'When you've finished your tea, will you go and get our Emma? I don't want her to be late. You know how time runs away from her, and I want us all there to see our Darren.'

'Do I have to?'

'Please.'

'OK. But there's hours yet.'

'Only three.' Vanessa grinned. 'I can't wait for it. To think the Sunderland coach is actually coming to watch our Darren... It ... it's amazing.'

'Yeah, but honestly, Mam, the thought of putting up with our Emma for the next three–'

'Shh,' Vanessa said as she turned the volume up.

The camera showed a shot of the shop in Houghton. There was very little to see – a policeman standing outside the doorway, and the windows boarded up. The announcer

155

said that the woman's name had not been given out yet until all the family had been informed, but that it was a pretty gruesome murder. The camera panned across the road where a group of people were standing, and the presenter walked over to them. He asked a woman, who Vanessa had never seen in Houghton before, if she knew the lady from the shop.

Shaking her head, she stepped back as Claire commented, 'My God, did you see the state of her lips? Looks like they've been blown up with a bicycle pump.'

But Vanessa was staring wide eyed at the screen, and a moment later, Claire gasped.

Standing next to three hoodies whose ages were hard to define, close to the woman with the huge lips, was Emma.

CHAPTER THIRTY-ONE

Lorraine left her mother and Peggy sitting with Luke, while she made her way down to the ground floor to visit Scottie's Domain, via the stairs. She hated using lifts, and had always had a fear of being stuck in one, especially by herself. The last thing she really wanted was to leave Luke's side, but she had to be doing something, anything, to get the crazy thought that Luke was going to die out of her mind.

Edna, well over retiring age, and who would more than likely die in her chair here rather than in some old people's home, was Scottie's right hand woman. She looked up from her microscope as Lorraine walked in.

'How is he, dear?' she asked, pushing her glasses to the top of her head. At the sound of her voice, Scottie, who had not heard Lorraine come in, turned towards them.

'No change, I'm afraid,' Lorraine said.

'Oh, dearie me. But he's strong, your Luke. Don't worry. I'm sure he'll pull through.'

Giving Edna a slight smile and a nod, Lorraine walked over to the table.

Scottie gave Lorraine a concerned glance. 'You don't have to do this, Lorraine.'

'Oh, but I do. I really need to keep occupied... So, tell me what you've found out so far.'

'If you're sure.'

Staring at the outline of the body under the white sheet, she paused for a moment. In her mind's eye, she could picture Luke lying as still as this poor woman. She mentally shook her head and pushed the image firmly away, before nodding at Scottie.

Gently, he pulled the sheet down over the body and, looking for a reaction from Lorraine, he said, 'Before you ask, Lorry, it's nowhere to be found.'

Lorraine sucked in a mouthful of air and tapped her fingers on the edge of the steel table, before saying, 'The cat?'

'No, it's a clean cut. Not a bite mark in sight.'

'I meant, could the cat have taken the hand somewhere? Hidden it? Put it wherever cats take their food?'

'I doubt that very much Lorraine. Take a look at this.' Scottie turned the woman's right hand over. There was a deep slash just above the wrist.

'Oh no... This is exactly what I didn't want. How come we didn't spot this at the murder scene?' Before Scottie could reply, she went on as she pictured the murder scene in her mind, 'Ah, yes. She was lying on her arm, wasn't she, so the missing hand couldn't be seen.'

'You thinking the same as me?'

Lifting her head, Lorraine looked at Scottie. 'Exactly what we don't want or need. He's a trophy taker.'

'Yes, that's what I thought. Somewhere there's another body with a missing right hand.'

'Yes. And how many other undiscovered bodies with missing pieces are there?'

'Aye, pet. I wondered that, an' all. And I'm certain that he got slightly confused with this one, and nearly cut the wrong hand off.'

Behind him, Edna shivered on her stool.

158

CHAPTER THIRTY-TWO

The heavy pounding on Sandra's door had lasted only for three minutes but crouched behind the door and praying that the lock didn't give, it felt like three hours to her.

Far from a coward, she wasn't stupid enough to take these three on single handedly, and the creep who knocked on her door had no soul in his eyes. She had never before felt so threatened by someone just looking at her.

Suddenly, there was silence. For a brief moment, this was worse than the deafening noise.

Where are they?

Have they gone round the back?

Slowly, Sandra rose up. Slipping her heels off and holding one aloft in her hand, she crept silently into the sitting room and peeked through the edge of the curtains.

Where the hell...?

She risked pulling the curtain further along, screamed and jumped back in shock. A muddy hand slapped the window three inches from her face, leaving the full imprint on the glass. Muddy water running down the imprint, like blood from a severed hand, freaked her out.

She thought her heart was going to burst, it was pounding so hard in her ears. Terrified she thought. What have I ever done to deserve this?

I've been a good person, helped people all my life. Yeah, told a few home truths in the past to those who needed it, but it mostly helped in the long run.

I know I've never deliberately hurt anyone.

She sighed, and it came from the bottom of her soul. This is truly what fear is.

A second later, his face was pressed against the window.

'Twenty-four fucking hours, missus, that's all you've got. This time tomorrow, bitch, or else. And it won't be you that fucking well gets it.' He laughed, a cruel heartless sound that set her teeth on edge.

She yanked the curtain back as hard as she could, and listened for the gate to close. She strained her ears, but there was no sound of the gate, so she figured they must have jumped over the wall. Unless they were waiting there to torment her even more.

Dare I risk looking out the window again?

What if they really haven't gone?

Taking a deep breath, she decided against it. She would give the bastards no chance to taunt her. She chewed on her fingernail for a moment – then gasped out loud. What did he mean by it won't be me?

Oh, God. No.

She pictured her boys as, one by one, their faces ran through her mind.

'No,' she muttered, hugging herself, 'please, not my boys.' Then louder. 'Not my boys!' The pain in her heart was so bad, she moaned out loud.

She had no intention of telling her family about the bother she was in. This was her mess, and she would sort it. She'd planned to get another loan out to pay this one off with, that had been her only hope, except that was dashed in a heartbeat. It had not been possible. The bank had refused.

And she should have realised this instead of getting her hopes up. The reason she'd made up her mind not to tell her family about her trouble was because the last thing she wanted was her boys themselves in trouble for fighting, or worse. No, she would sort this herself. Many a time, a good kid has been locked up for life defending his family, and her four boys were her life. She worshipped each and every one. If anything happened to any of them, it would be the death of her.

She suddenly remembered, with a rush of fear up her spine, that the back door was unlocked.

'Shit... Shit... Shit...' Grabbing her shoe back up, she ran to the kitchen, panicking in case they had silently come in that way. She slammed the bolt home, and took a deep breath, looking quickly around in case, God forbid, she'd locked them in with her.

'Oh, my God. What if they're hiding up the stairs?'

She looked for muddy marks on the floor. In the hallway, she fell to her knees, desperately rubbing her hands over the carpet, feeling for damp spots that shoes would make.

CHAPTER THIRTY-THREE

Back in Luke's room, Lorraine took the files she'd brought from the station out of her bag. Her mother sat on one side of Luke's bed, writing a shopping list for Peggy. Suddenly she looked up.

'Lorry, did you tell Selina about her dad?'

'Yes. I wasn't sure but,' she looked over at Luke, 'I thought it best. They're getting the two-thirty train home.'

'You did the right thing, love.' Mavis smiled at her.

'I know. But such a shame, their first holiday together. Especially as he's gonna be all right,' she said with conviction.

Standing up, she walked over to the bed

and took hold of Luke's hand. 'You are going to be all right, aren't you Luke?'

'Course he is. You got that list done yet, Mave?' Peggy said.

'Just about.' A moment later she tore the sheet of paper off the writing pad Lorraine had given her, and handed it over. 'Here, and don't forget anything.'

'As if.' Peggy took the sheet of paper, and ran her eyes over the list. 'OK, I'm on it.' She threw Mavis a salute and headed out the door, saying, 'Don't do anything I wouldn't do.'

'As if,' Mavis replied, giving her a sweet smile.

Lorraine shook her head. 'She gets no better.'

'That's Peggy for you. Life is one big joke. Too damn late for her to change now. But I think I'll have a word with her about Sandy, she teases him relentlessly, poor soul.'

'You think having a word will make any difference?'

Mavis sighed. 'Not really.'

A moment later they both froze, then swung their heads towards Luke. Lorraine's heart skipped a beat.

'You ... you heard it as well, didn't you, Mam? Please say you did. Please.'

'Yes.'

Lorraine quickly moved to Luke's side and took hold of his hand. 'Luke? Luke, please wake up.'

For a moment there was silence. Then they both heard it again. Luke groaned, very quietly, and this time moved his head.

'Get the doctor, Mam, quick.'

Mavis jumped up and went into the corridor. She grabbed a passing nurse by her arm. 'Please, come quick. He moved his head. Where's the doctor?'

'I'll page him, but first, let's take a look.'

She followed Mavis back into the room.

A few seconds later, Luke opened his eyes.

'Oh, Luke!' Lorraine cried, as tears ran down her face.

The nurse who had taken Luke's temperature smiled. 'Well now, that's well down.'

'Thank God,' Mavis said quietly.

'What ... where...'

Lorraine grabbed his hand and squeezed, her heart filling when a few moments later he squeezed back. She leaned close to him and whispered, 'I love you, Luke.'

Just then, the doctor came in. After checking him over, he said, 'Well, I can definitely say you are on the mend. Another day in here with complete bed rest and you'll be able to go home. Nurse?' He turned to the nurse. 'You can take him off everything. Keep the paracetamol going for the next twelve hours and that should be it.'

'Yes, doctor.'

Lorraine could only stare in wonderment

at Luke. He had closed his eyes again, and was probably dozing, but he was going to live. He was going to be all right!

Finishing up, the nurse left them, smiling at Lorraine as she moved from the bed.

'I'll pop out for a bit, give youse guys some time alone.' Mavis put her arms around her daughter and hugged her.

'Thanks, Mam.'

Luke moaned, louder this time, and opened his eyes again. Frowning at Lorraine, he struggled to sit up.

'Now, wait a minute.' Standing up, Lorraine plumped his pillows and helped him ease himself up. 'That's enough for today, OK?'

Luke sighed. 'What the hell happened?'

'Don't you know?'

'Would I be asking?'

'Well, if you don't know, nobody else does.'

Luke's frown deepened. 'Lorry, what the hell's been going on, why am I...?'

Just then the doctor came back into the room carrying a folder with Luke's name written on it. His attitude towards Luke had totally changed, as he said abruptly, 'What sort of drugs do you take?'

'Drugs!' Lorraine and Luke said in unison.

'Yes, that's what I said.'

'No way, Doctor. I do not under any circumstances take any drugs of any kind.'

'Well, your blood tests have just come back,

showing a mishmash of quite a few substances.'

Amazed Luke looked at Lorraine and slowly shook his head.

Squeezing Luke's hand tightly, Lorraine turned to the doctor. 'Something must be wrong, Doctor, because my Luke is not a drug addict. To be fair, would a druggie have survived what he just has?'

'To be fair, I very much doubt it. But there must be a reason for all of these toxins in his bloodstream.'

Lorraine looked at Luke. 'He has a point. Where the hell did they come from?'

'I have no idea at all.' Luke struggled to sit further up. 'But the bastard who put them there is certainly gonna suffer. Can I have a mirror?'

'You don't really want one.'

Luke carefully touched his nose, then slowly nodded his head. 'Oh, but I do.'

The nurse came in with a fresh jug of water, and the doctor said, 'Whatever, however, wherever they came from, I want you to drink as much fluid as you can.'

Luke nodded. 'Yes, thank you.' He turned back to Lorraine. 'What the hell happened?'

'We don't know. Luke, I was worried sick when I didn't hear anything from you.'

'Not even a trifle angry?' Luke said, with a wry smile.

'Well, a bit... OK then, a big bit.'

'That's my girl.'

Lorraine pulled a face. 'OK, there's a few things you need to know and a few things I need to know, before I let them know at the station that you're awake and out of danger.'

Luke was quiet for a minute, digesting what Lorraine had said, and had the feeling that what she hadn't yet said did not bode well, especially for him.

'Please, Lorraine, start at the beginning. I need to know everything and don't sweeten the pill.'

'OK.' Taking hold of his hand, which actually did nothing to allay Luke's fears, she went on. 'The first thing we heard was when Rosie came to the station to tell me you'd turned up on her doorstep with Len and Danny Jordan propping you up. And that's about all we really know. We have no idea where you spent the night, only that it had to have been outside. Our guess so far is, seeing as your phone, wallet, and watch are missing, and by the state of your face, you were beaten up.'

Slowly, Luke shook his head. 'Don't remember seeing Rosie or any of the others... Last thing I remember was coming out of the Beehive.'

'You sure?'

Luke frowned. 'Yes.'

'There's something else.'

With a sinking heart, Luke said, 'Shit...

What sort of something else?'

'Did you drive your car away from the Beehive?'

CHAPTER THIRTY-FOUR

He opened his eyes again.

He was cold.

Freezing cold.

He tried to move, but again the pain was so intense that he groaned loudly.

He felt something brush past his face, and his heart was once more flooded with fear.

Spiders?

Rats!

He sobbed. He was never going to get out of here.

CHAPTER THIRTY-FIVE

Vanessa and Claire were waiting at the bus stop, for the bus to Houghton.

'Where the fuck is it?' Vanessa looked up the street for the ninth time in as many minutes. 'I swear, I'll strangle the little shit, going up to Houghton by herself.'

'She's a thicko all right, Mam, standing grinning in front of the cameras as if no one would recognise her.'

Vanessa shook her head. 'If our Kerry sees her up there, she'll get a clip round the ear hole all right. She'll not be so flaming cocky then. And who the hell were those three creeps she was standing next to?'

Claire was busy checking her red painted nails for chips.

'Well? Do you know them, or not?' Vanessa demanded.

'Who?

'Oh, for God's sake Claire. Them three on the telly, next to our Emma.'

'Oh, them, right. One was that horrible Stevie Masterton, and one was friggin Fartin' Martin. Haven't got a clue who the other one was.'

'Who?'

'Never mind. Martin Raynor.'

'So why call him Fa–'

'Never mind,' Claire cut in, before she could say any more. Vanessa frowned at her. 'I'm only asking.'

'I know. Sorry, Mam. Maybes we should have walked up. I hate waiting around like this.'

'If we start now, the stupid bus will come.'

Claire sighed. 'Don't even know why we're haring up there for, anyhow. She's probably on her way back down. In fact she's prob-

169

ably watching the telly.'

'And she's probably not. I've never seen that other bloke about. And neither have you... God knows who he is. Could be an axe murderer, for all we know. An escapee from the nut house, who friggin knows.'

'Mam!'

Claire knew that what had happened to her last year had made their mother a nervous wreck whenever one of them was late for any reason. But, as Doris had said, every cloud has a silver lining, and what had happened had been one of the prime reasons their mother was now sober.

The bus finally arrived. Vanessa paid the fares, complaining the whole time about the price for only two stops. The bus driver shrugged. He'd heard it all before. 'Nowt to do with me, missus, I just drive the bus.'

A few minutes later, they got off the bus in the middle of Houghton. Of the TV cameras there was no sign, and the crowd that had been hanging around were long gone.

Vanessa and Claire crossed the road and went into the paper shop. Kerry was busy stocking the shelves with chocolate bars. Looking up, she spotted her mother and Claire and waved them down to the back of the shop.

'What's up?' She frowned at them.

'Our Emma was on the telly,' Claire quickly said.

'No way.'

'Way.'

'I saw the cameras.' Kerry glanced at her mother, noticing how pale she looked. 'Don't worry, Mam, I looked up the street. There was loads of people standing there. It's not every day the cameras come here, you know.' She laughed, 'This is Houghton not London.'

'But she knows she's not allowed up Houghton by herself. She's too young to go flitting about here and there. And I'm guessing she hasn't been in here.'

'Sorry, haven't clapped eyes on her. Look, just forget it, will you? She'll be back home by now. I don't even know why you're worrying.'

'That's what I said,' Claire nodded. 'Come on, Mam, let's get home. I'm bored already.'

'Oh, can't you find anything else to say but "I'm bored"?'

Claire shrugged. 'Not really.' She headed for the doorway as she pulled her phone out and started texting.

Watching her, Vanessa shook her head, and looked at Kerry. 'I guess in a way she's right. I overreacted again.'

Kerry touched her mother's arm. 'Forget it, eh? Just ground the little witch when she comes home.'

'OK, pet... Shepherd's pie for tea?'

'Great! Only–'

'I know. Leave a piece with no cheese on.' Vanessa smiled as she followed Claire out the door.

Watching her, Kerry felt a lump in her throat. Her Mam had had a terrible life. And now she was trying so hard, but freaking out at the smallest thing. Was there something they didn't know about? Something else hidden away deep in their mother's past? Something zooming in like a rocket hell bent on destruction. She shook her head.

'No way.' she muttered, picking the box of chocolate bars up. 'We've had far more than our share of bad luck already, more than a lifetime's.'

CHAPTER THIRTY-SIX

Luke stared at Lorraine. 'What do you mean? From what I can remember, I was in no fit state to drive a flaming scooter never mind a car.'

'Only...'

'Only what?'

Lorraine took a deep breath. 'Only your car was used in a hit and run in the middle of last night, or the early hours of this morning, whichever way you want to put it.' Knowing she was babbling, Lorraine shut up and reached for Luke's hand. He snatched it away. If she thought Luke hadn't looked well before, he looked ghastly now. Self-consciously, she put her hand in her pocket.

'You ... you think it was me.'

'No. No, I don't. No one thinks it was you.'

He looked at her, then transferred his gaze to the window. 'Tell me.'

'A young girl was murdered.'

'Murdered? How?'

'Some bastard driving your car ran her down, then reversed over her. Which basically means that, because it's your car, you are the prime suspect... For fuck's sake, you know how it works.'

'I'm gonna be sick.'

Lorraine grabbed a round cardboard sick tray from the night stand and put it in his hands. Luke swallowed hard and managed to keep it down. He rested his head on the pillow for a moment until the dizziness passed.

Knowing that there wasn't much time, and that Fyfe had probably already found out that Luke was greatly improved, and would without doubt be coming in herself to question him, she said, 'Luke, it's really important. What can you remember?'

'Not a lot.' He sighed. 'Who is she? Do I ... do I know her?'

'I doubt it very much. But I need to know everything that you did. Please – can you

173

remember anything at all?'

'Like driving the car, you mean.'

'That was a low shot, Luke.'

'Just go.'

'What?' Lorraine couldn't believe what he had just said.

'Lorraine, you're questioning me like you really think I would do something like that. Just go.'

'I'm sorry, Luke, but this is the way Fyfe will question you. Luke?' She reached for his hand again. 'I love you, and I swear I never once thought you capable of anything like this.'

This time Luke did not rebuff her hand. Instead, he held on, and looked into her eyes. His own were filled with a deep sadness and an underlying worry.

'I'm sorry, Lorraine. It's all just been a bit of a shock. I don't know...'

She nodded. 'OK, don't worry. We will get to the bottom of this, I promise. Now please, you must try to remember what happened last night.'

'OK.' He closed his eyes for a few minutes. When he opened them, he said, 'I remember being in the Beehive, and Sanderson singing ... oh yes, it was more like torturing, some Bee Gees song.'

'It will have been *Staying Alive*. His favourite.'

Luke gave a slow nod. 'Then two or three

young men wearing hoodies came in, and suddenly they were practically sitting on my knee.'

Lorraine frowned. 'Can you remember what they looked like at all, even one of them?'

'Not really. I guess if I saw them again, I might.'

'Were they there long enough to nick your car keys?'

'I think so.'

'It's got to be them, then.'

'But why?'

'I talked this over with Sanderson. We thought it could be a revenge killing. Either someone stole your car to implicate you, or your car was in the wrong place at the wrong time. Me, I think it's the former.'

'Some creep seeking revenge because I banged the low life bastard up?'

'Yes.'

'So, how we gonna prove it wasn't me driving?'

'Leave it with me. I've just had an idea...'

'So, this is nice and cosy.' DI Alison Fyfe walked in to the room and stood at the end of Luke's bed. 'How are you, Detective Sergeant Daniels?'

Before Luke could answer, she turned to Lorraine. 'I thought you were told to keep away from the case.'

'I can hardly be expected to keep away

from my own fiancé, can I now?'

'Fiancé? Since when?' Fyfe snapped, a sneer on her face.

'Since now.' Luke smiled, and took Lorraine's hand.

CHAPTER THIRTY-SEVEN

When Vanessa and Claire got off the bus back home, Vanessa said, 'I'm popping along to Sandra's for a bit. If Madam comes in, do not let her out. I mean it.'

'OK.' Tapping away on her phone, Claire walked up the street towards their house.

Tutting, Vanessa went in the opposite direction, wondering what the hell would happen if all mobile phones suddenly died for a whole month. 'The kids would shoot themselves,' she muttered. Shaking her head, she carried on, thinking that on her way back from Sandra's, she would call in and see how Doris was doing.

Reaching Sandra's house, she was surprised to see the curtains drawn. Wearing a puzzled frown, she walked down the path, reaching for the handle and turning. Surprise number two – Sandra's door was locked. She knocked, then again. Still no answer. Bending down, she opened the letterbox and was about to shout, when she thought she heard someone crying.

'What?' she whispered to herself. 'No. I'm hearing things.'

Then the crying sound came again.

'Sandra? Sandra, is that you in there? Answer me... Sandra!'

For a moment, Vanessa could hear nothing. She was about to shout again when she heard, 'Yes, it's me. I'm coming.'

Vanessa got a shock a moment later, when the letterbox opened and she could see Sandra peering out. 'What the...?'

'Is there anyone else out there?'

Vanessa looked around, and said with a small laugh, 'Ain't nobody here but us chickens, missus.'

'Is there anyone in the streets? Young 'uns with hoodies on? Please, look properly, Vanessa.'

Frowning, Vanessa looked around again. 'No, there's no one else here. For God's sake, stop taking the piss and let me in.'

Sandra took the locks off and opened the door. Quickly she grabbed Vanessa's arm and pulled her inside.

'What the...?'

Sandra said nothing until she had finished relocking the door, which freaked Vanessa out. Then she practically forced Vanessa into a chair by the fire, and sat in the one facing her. 'I ... I'm in trouble,' was as far as she got before she buried her head in her hands and burst into tears.

Vanessa was shocked. Sandra was the strong one, she always had been. Jumping up, she crossed over and, sitting on the arm of the chair, she put her arm across Sandra's shoulders.

'What the hell's wrong?'

'I ... I'm in deep shit, Vanessa, really bad.'

'Nowt's that bad.'

'Oh, it is.' She started to cry again.

'For pity's sake, just tell me.'

Sandra looked up at Vanessa. 'OK ... OK, I will.'

It took a few minutes, but when she'd finished Vanessa sat back in amazement. 'Well,' she finally managed. 'What the hell can I say, except I'm fucking gob-smacked?'

'What am I gonna do?'

'Tell them to fuck off.'

Sandra shook her head, and replied in a small voice, 'I can't.'

'Sandra! You're not scared of Stevie Masterton and his shit of a friend, Martin. I don't believe it.'

'It's not them.'

'Who is it, then?'

'The other one. The new one. I'm telling you, Vanessa, he's evil. Pure evil. It's what he might do to my boys that I'm more scared of.'

'So who is he?'

'I heard one of them call him Dev as they left.'

'Is that short for devil?'

Sandra shivered. 'Not funny, Vanessa.'

'Sorry. So how much is this payment?'

'A hundred.'

'Pounds!'

Sandra just looked at her.

'OK, but haven't you got it?' She looked around the room. Sandra had always had great taste, and in here Vanessa had always felt that she was a million miles away from the Seahills, in some luxury hotel.

'Not until next week. But they won't wait.'

'Well, they'll fucking well have to... For God's sake, Sandra, since when have you been frightened of punks like them?'

Sandra shook her head and flopped back in her chair.

'Wait a minute. Why haven't you got it? You've never been short of a bob or two before.'

'I did explain.'

Vanessa sighed. There was nothing she could do to help, certainly not cash-wise. But I still can't understand how she's broke. Sandra's never broke.

'So where we gonna get a hundred quid by tomorrow?'

Sandra shook her head. 'What am I gonna do?' she wailed.

'Sell something.' Vanessa looked around.

'Come on. Sandra, there must be some of this stuff worth money.'

'I suppose.'

'It's a way out. I know you love your things, but needs must. Have a sort out.'

Sandra nodded, a faint glimmer of hope on her face.

She would do it.

It was a way out.

She heaved a sigh of relief. For the first time in hours, her heart rate settled down and the headache seemed to ease.

'Oh shit. What the hell time did they say they were coming?' Vanessa asked.

'In the morning, half past eleven.'

'OK. I'll be here first thing, as soon as I get the troops up and off, and we'll go to the pawn shop, that one in Sunderland. We should get there and back in time. If we offer Jacko some petrol money, then we'll definitely make it... Hang on a minute. I've just realised who them three punks were, standing beside our Emma. Stevie Masterton, Martin Raynor, and that other must have been that Dev person.'

'Where?'

Vanessa had not told Sandra about Emma being on the television until now. When she had finished, Sandra said, 'She wouldn't have been with them. I mean, why would she? Why would they want to knock around with a kid?' She was praying that she was

180

right. The last thing Vanessa needed was for Emma to go astray. Things were just getting on track for her.

'You're probably right, and I panicked for nothing. Anyhow, gotta get back, make sure everybody's smart and clean for our Darren's football. You still coming?'

Sandra sighed. Really, it was the last place she wanted to be, but she had promised Darren. 'OK. There's nowt else I can do, is there? I might as well be with your lot, shouting him on.'

'That's a girl. We'll give you a knock on the way. Have a cup of tea, and I'll see meself out. And stop worrying. You know what they say, you can't get blood out of a stone. And the rest of it, we'll sort. Don't worry.'

CHAPTER THIRTY-EIGHT

Sanderson and Dinwall made good time up to Galashiels. It took them a while to find Tweed Cottage. When they did, it was an eighteenth century two up, two down, in the middle of nowhere, with what looked like climbing roses covering the whole length and breadth of the walls – though in deep December, there wasn't a rose in sight. Still, Sanderson thought, I bet it's a fantastic display in the summer.

'Come on, then. I do want to get back to civilisation by midnight at the latest.' Dinwall opened the gate.

'Shut up. It's barely gone three.'

'Aye, but there's bound to be heavy traffic on the way back. And getting past that Metro Centre between five and seven this time of year, it's practically impossible.'

'Come on, then. And thank God this house isn't in the middle of Edinburgh or somewhere. Then you would really know what a traffic jam is.' Sanderson hated to be the bearer of bad news. Not that they were in this case – the Galashiels police had already seen to that.

Dinwall knocked on the door. He was about to knock again when the door was opened by a small blonde woman. He was thinking that she must have seen them coming up the long path between two lawns, to answer it so quickly.

Sanderson introduced himself and Dinwall. The woman, whose eyes were red from crying, was dressed in a green jumper and a tartan skirt. She looked Sanderson up and down. She must have liked what she saw, as she opened the door before he got his credentials out.

'I've been expecting you,' she said, in a small, sad voice. 'That nice policeman from town told us. Please come in.'

They followed her down a long narrow corridor and entered a room on their right. Two men, obviously father and son, and a young woman were seated in various positions around the bright airy room. The walls were pale cream and hung with many landscape paintings, in direct contrast to the oppressive hallway. Dinwall was right in thinking that those gathered there were part of the dead woman's family.

'It's that bastard. I know it is,' said the young man, jumping up from his chair by the window. He was fair haired, with a thin moustache, and dressed in jeans and a blue t-shirt.

'Who?' Sanderson asked, as he sat in the red plush chair indicated by the woman.

'The one she left home for. The bastard she left her own family for, to go down to friggin' England.'

His mother tufted. 'Really, James, you should at least give the gentlemen a chance to get seated. And please rein in your language.'

'Sorry, Ma.' Scowling, the young man sat down again.

'Well, first, can I say we are sorry for your loss.' Sanderson said. The older man, bald and slightly overweight, nodded at him. 'And we're here to try and find out as much as we can about your daughter, and any contacts she may have had, friends, relationships.' Sanderson took out his notebook.

'It's him, I'm telling you.'

'James!' His mother glared at him, as his father gripped the arms of his chair.

'Who do you mean by "him"?' Dinwall asked.

Pleased that someone was finally taking notice of him, James said, 'Her lorry driver boyfriend.'

'Do you have a name for him?' Sanderson asked.

'You see, that's just it, we haven't. She never did tell us his name. Never once mentioned it, even though we kept asking her. The fact that he was a lorry driver was something we only found out by chance.'

Sanderson turned to the sister. Her hair was a dark golden colour, and she wore a navy skirt suit, with a white blouse. Sanderson guessed she worked in an office. She shook her head. 'She didn't tell me his name either, even though I kept asking an' all,' she said, before Sanderson asked her. Her face changed colour, and she turned to look at her mother.

'Lately, our Stella and our Karen didn't get on too well, officer. They, er ... they had a major row just before our Karen moved away.'

'Can you tell me what about?' Sanderson turned back to Stella.

Stella sighed. 'Him, that's what it was

about. He ruled her life. The jerk was a control freak, but she wouldn't have it. She thought the sun shone out of his arse. She should have listened to me. I had the drift of him, right off.'

'Hmm. So, seeing as none of you met him, you can't give me a description.'

'I know for a fact she only ever fancied men with really dark hair, and they had to be tall.'

'And that's probably at least seventy percent of the male population,' Dinwall put in, nodding his head. 'That have dark hair, I mean.'

Sanderson closed his notebook. 'So the only thing you can give me is that he was a lorry driver. Any idea which firm he worked for?'

They all shook their heads. James said. 'The bloke was a creep, officer, but our Karen wouldn't listen to us. We tried our best. It's like she was brainwashed. She made herself a stranger, and there was nothing we could do. She even threatened to get the coppers on me once.'

'Oh? And why was that?' Sanderson raised his eyebrows.

'Just ...well, just because I threatened to have him sorted.'

'And did you? Have him sorted?' Dinwall asked.

James shrugged. 'How could I? Didn't

have a clue who the hell he was.'

'OK, then. Thanks for your help.' Declining the cup of tea that the mother offered, Sanderson rose and followed by Dinwall, was led to the door by James.

'Mind you catch the bastard, officer,' he said to them.

'We will do our best, but we really don't have a lot to go on. Here,' he took a card out of his top pocket, 'if any of you remember anything, no matter how small, ring me.'

'Sure.' James took the card, turned it over and studied what was written there. 'Goodbye.' Slowly, he closed the door.

'Well,' Dinwall stated as they walked down the path.

Sanderson waited until they were in the car before saying, 'Well, indeed.'

'I reckon it could have been him, the brother.'

'What makes you think that?' Sanderson started the car, and headed for home.

'His attitude. And it's a proven fact that you're more likely to be murdered by someone you know, rather than a stranger.'

'OK. So what about the father? Pretty strange he never said a word.'

'No, not him, probably he was still in shock... Or, maybes he knows it's his son.'

'Or maybes we're just jumping to conclusions.' Sanderson pulled up outside of a catering van. 'Cup of tea and a bacon sarnie, please.'

Grumbling about wasting time, Dinwall got out of the car.

CHAPTER THIRTY-NINE

'So you couldn't even do the first fucking job I send you on properly. Not good enough.'

Dev shrugged. 'Got half the money in, didn't we? You want miracles, or what?' He glared at her.

'Not good enough,' she repeated, then turned to Stevie. 'Thought you had a word with him?'

'I did. But ha'way, man, give us a chance. Not all of the punters were in, and some we have to go back to tomorrow.'

She looked at her hands and stretched her fingers. The very action sent shivers down Martin's back.

'OK. One chance, and one only. But I want youse back on the job tomorrow. In the meantime...' She opened the bottom drawer of her desk, reached in and pulled out five packets of pills. 'Get to work on these. I spent a couple of months in Russia perfecting these with a few friends of mine. It was known, I suppose still is, as Krokodil. Mostly injected, because it's dirt cheap.' She

187

laughed. 'It's made of dirt, as well.' Finding this funny, she laughed some more.

'Right.' Stevie and Dev reached for the packets, while Martin stared at them as if he was in a trance. He'd heard about Krokodil, the drug that eats you from the inside, made from a concoction of petrol and other obnoxious substances. Once on that train, you were on a ride straight to hell. And she had now made it much easier to get hooked.

'What's the matter with that fucking idiot? Hey, you! Give the dozy twat a poke.'

'He's all right, ain't yer?' Stevie quickly did as she said and poked Martin in his ribs.

Martin gulped. 'What ... what?'

'Wake up, dickhead.'

How the hell am I gonna get out of this? She won't give a flying fuck what happens to the people who get addicted to her poison.

How the hell am I even gonna get out of what happened last night?

He looked at the packets of pills, then up at Mrs Archer. Whatever she was calling herself now, she would always be Mrs Archer to him.

'Well, get a fucking move on!' she screamed at him. 'And these are not for the kids. Never kill the food chain off. There's plenty for them to be trying before they need this stuff.'

Martin could hear Dev sniggering. He reached for the last packet and put them in his pocket. He knew then that he was truly lost. There would never be a way out for him.

There was no hope left.

He was already an accomplice to murder, and he still couldn't get straight in his head just exactly what had happened. Stevie had picked out the wrong girl that was for sure. Everything else was a frightened blur.

Five minutes later, they were heading towards the dole centre.

'So, what you planning on doing?' Stevie asked, walking side by side with Dev, with Martin as usual trailing behind.

'I'll tell you when you fucking need to know, OK? For now, we've got some money to make. And we've got some people to upset when we muscle in on their trade, so we might as well start now with the lowlifes.'

'About that... There's some pretty hard people around here, and they ain't gonna like what you've got planned, and that's a fact believe me.'

'Really, now?' Dev grinned. 'Bothered?'

'You should be,' Stevie said quietly.

'What did you say?' Dev turned and, before Stevie had a chance to move, Dev grabbed him by his throat.

'Just what sort of fucking coward are you, eh? Eh?'

'I'm not, I'm not a fucking coward. Who do think I am, fuckin' Fartin'? I'm just try-ing to warn you, that's all.'

Dev let go of him. 'Like I already said, we'll deal with things as they come.' He stared at Stevie. 'Do those fucking rings in your face not get on your fucking nerves?'

'Not really.' Pleased that Dev had changed the subject, he went on, 'Never fancied any yourself? I know a guy who does them on the cheap, like.'

'Fuck off.' He turned to Martin, only he wasn't there. Dev spun round in a full circle, as did Stevie. 'The bastard! He's fucking done a runner.'

They looked at each other. 'Mrs Archer isn't gonna like this one fucking bit,' Stevie said.

CHAPTER FORTY

Vanessa opened the kitchen door. She dreaded going inside, in case Emma wasn't back, and instead of coming straight back from Sandra's, she'd gone past the swing park only to find it empty. But the first thing she saw was Emma treating herself to a bag of crisps. The feeling of relief that overwhelmed her nearly made her knees buckle.

Quickly pulling herself together she said, 'Ah, the film star's back... What the hell were you doing up Houghton, Madam?'

Emma turned to her mother and grinned. 'I was on the telly.'

'Yes, we all know that.'

Emma shrugged. 'I found a fifty pence, so I–'

'I don't care if you found a fifty pound note. You are not allowed up Houghton by yourself. You know this, Emma.'

Claire shouted from the hallway, 'What's all the noise about now?' She walked into the kitchen and spotted Emma. 'Oh. It's you. Back, I see.'

'I was on the telly.'

Claire pulled a face at her before turning to her mother. 'So what time we going to this stupid football match then?'

'I was on the telly.'

'We'll be going as soon as the others get in, about ten minutes or so.'

'I was on the telly.' Emma shouted this time.

Both of them turned to her. 'Yes, you were. And what were you doing with Stevie Masterton and the other two creeps?' Claire demanded.

'Who?'

Claire raised her eyes towards the ceiling, and sighed. 'Stop pretending you're thick, our Emma.'

'Well, if she's thick or not, you,' she turned to Emma, 'are grounded.'

'What for?' Emma said, tears coming to

her eyes.

'You know what for. Now get upstairs and change your clothes.'

'Do I have to?' Emma scowled.

Vanessa moved towards her.

'OK, OK, I'm going.' Emma shuffled off the stool and ran as fast as she could for the stairs.

A few minutes later Robbie came in, followed by Kerry. Robbie had filled out and was now close to six foot. Vanessa was so proud of him. So kind, so caring, even after everything that had happened. Many a lad his age would have taken off, but not him. Robbie had stood by them all.

'If anybody else tells me this day that our Emma's been on the telly, I'll scream,' Kerry said, putting her navy sports bag under the kitchen bench. 'That's all I've heard all flaming day, people coming into the shop one after the other. "Eee' I saw your Emma on the telly..." Where is she?'

'Getting changed, and you'll no doubt hear all about it from the film star herself.'

'I'm next for the bathroom,' Robbie said, running out of the kitchen and taking the stairs three at a time.

'Damn.' Kerry stamped her foot.

'I was on the telly,' Emma said to Robbie, as she came out of the bedroom and he reached the top of the stairs.

He ruffled her hair as he disappeared into

the bathroom. 'Well done, kiddo.'

'Can't wait to tell our Darren,' she said on her way downstairs. She had changed into a pair of Claire's old jeans, which were a bit tight round the waist. She ran her thumb round the waistband, thinking if she could find the scissors, she just might be able to cut a notch or two. Emma was quite chubby, not that it ever bothered her. She had a blue jumper on that also belonged to Claire.

Our Claire never wears them now, so she shouldn't moan about it, she was thinking as she entered the kitchen. Before she could say anything, she had Claire's finger pressed against her lips. 'Don't even think about it.'

'OK.' When Claire turned away, Emma pulled a face behind Claire's back. 'You're just jealous, anyhow.'

'All right, stop it now, the pair of you... And I want best behaviour at the game today, I mean it. We want our Darren to be as proud of us as we are of him,' Vanessa said, raising her eyebrows at Emma. If Claire hadn't noticed what Emma was wearing, she certainly had.

Fifteen minutes later, they headed for Sandra's house. When they reached her gate, Emma skipped in front and ran to the door. When Sandra opened it, she said, 'I was–'

'On the telly,' Sandra interrupted with a

smile, as she bent over and kissed the top of Emma's head.

Pleased to see that Sandra looked a bit better, Vanessa linked arms with her friend and they all headed off to the school.

CHAPTER FORTY-ONE

He opened his eyes. Hunger flared in his stomach.

Where am I?

This time he remembered being awake before. He licked his dry lips, and realised he was as thirsty as he was hungry.

'Help!' he cried, but it was very feeble and barely above a whisper.

Again he slipped into unconsciousness. Just before the dark closed in again, he thought he saw a familiar face. But putting a name to the face was impossible.

CHAPTER FORTY-TWO

Lorraine put her phone down and looked at Luke who, thank God, she thought, seemed to be improving by the hour.

Fyfe had left forty minutes ago, and the guard was still out there. Having agreed that the evidence was circumstantial, Luke had not been arrested, but Lorraine could tell that Fyfe was out to nail him.

As if sensing her staring at him, Luke opened his eyes. 'Has she truly gone?'

'Yeah, but she'll be back.'

'Thanks for that.'

Lorraine shrugged. 'If you could only remember what the hell happened...'

'Don't you think I've tried? The last thing I can see are those three hoodies.'

'They are out looking for them, but your description could fit half the youths ... men ... boys in England.'

'Think its time I got out of here.' He threw the covers back, then collapsed into a coughing fit.

'No way.' Lorraine covered him up. 'You might be on the mend, but it's early days yet. And you are not to even attempt to get out of bed until tomorrow at the earliest.

That's the doc's orders, and mine.'

Luke sighed. 'Did any one ever tell you before that you're a right bossy bitch?'

'Yes, you, more than once.'

Luke gave her a weak smile.

'Right then, seeing as you're a tad better, and to save you sinking into total boredom and starting to consider escape plans, I'm going to pick your brains.'

'OK, lovely, pick away.' He smiled, thankful that he would have something to concentrate on, to give his subconscious time to come up with some answers.

'There was some thought that both murders could be connected. I personally doubt that very much.'

Luke mulled it over. 'Time scale?'

'Well, it's doable, seeing as it's probably only a five minute walk, ten at the most, from Houghton Cut to Newbottle Street.'

'So if Fyfe has her way, she'll have me down for both murders. Nice.'

'Luke, everyone in the station knows it's not you.' She took hold of his hand.

'Yeah, so you say. But it's proving it.'

'Yes, but the blood tests have more or less proven that you were totally incapable of looking after yourself, never mind committing two murders.'

He squeezed her hand. 'Let's hope so.'

'Right, then. I've just had a phone call from Sanderson. I sent him and Dinwall up to Galashiels, to talk to the family, and Dinwall seems adamant that it's her brother.'

Luke raised his eyebrows. 'Not unknown... But why? There has to be a reason.'

'Seems he's, according to Dinwall, "shifty eyed and a bully". Sanderson isn't saying no, though he doubts it.'

'Bring him in. Won't do any harm to talk to him.'

'The order's on its way. The Galashiels police have been great in all of this, and they're gonna bring him down.'

Luke started sneezing. Lorraine stuffed half a dozen paper handkerchiefs into his hand. After a minute, he lay back. She could see he was worn out already. 'Tell you what, I'll leave you to rest for a while, OK? I'll be back later.'

He barely nodded as his eyes closed. Lorraine got quietly up, filled his glass full of orange juice, then slung the strap of her handbag over her shoulder and headed for the lift at the end of the corridor.

She called a cab at the hospital gates and directed him to her mother's house. She would have a bite to eat, take the dog for a walk, and mull over everything she knew so far, before catching up with Sanderson and Dinwall – and waiting to hear from Carter what he'd learned from Fyfe's squad.

CHAPTER FORTY-THREE

At the school gates Vanessa, her family and Sandra waited for the youngest Lumsden. Suzy, who wearing a brand new uniform and, for once, not a cast-off from her sister, came quite happily skipping down the path.

'I was on the telly,' Emma shouted, just before Suzy reached them.

'Was not.' Suzy stopped dead in amazement.

'Was too.' Emma grinned at her.

'Was she really on the telly?' Suzy took hold of her mother's hand as she looked up, disbelief on her face. Smiling, Vanessa nodded at her.

'Wow.'

'Yes, definitely wow, and I doubt we've heard the last of it. Come on then, all, over to the sports field.' With a smile on her face, Vanessa put her shoulders back and, with her family in tow, walked proudly over the yard.

As they crossed the yard and went behind the school towards the sport field, Sandra put on a brave face. It was probably the best day that Vanessa had had for years, and no way was she going to spoil it with her own problems.

They stood in a line at the edge of the field, all of them proudly waiting for Darren to show. Vanessa had wondered at the strange looks she'd received from the head-master and the sports teacher, but shrugged them off. They're probably wondering who I am. Either that, or they don't believe I've managed to turn the corner, she thought, watching the team make their way onto the pitch.

Robbie's heart swelled with pride. His brother Darren was going to go far, definitely way far. When that scout clocks him, he's in for a shock. Darren is one hell of a footballer, and actually should have been picked up before. But the chance was here now. He tried to wipe the grin off his face, but it wouldn't go away.

Kerry pictured her brother in years to come striding down the pitch with the ball at his feet, adoring fans screaming for him to score. She too felt as if her heart would burst with pride.

Little Suzy was jumping up and down, repeating her brother's name over and over. When the team lined up, facing the oppo-sition, she said loudly what everyone else was wondering: 'Where's our Darren?'

Vanessa glanced at Sandra, and frowning, mouthed, 'Where the hell is he?'

Sandra shrugged, then said, 'Best ask the sports teacher, or the headmaster. Look, he's coming over.'

Reaching them, the headmaster, a tall thin man with a really deep voice, said, 'You are aware, Mrs Lumsdon, that Darren has not been in school all day?'

Vanessa felt her heart gripped by hands of ice cold steel.

It was Kerry who found her voice first. 'What do you mean, he's not here? He set out this morning excited to death.'

'Yes, he has been excited all week. But I'm afraid, as you can see, much to our surprise and, obviously, yours,' he looked back at the team, 'he's not here.'

'So.' Robbie said. 'He's been missing all day, and you never thought to phone.'

'I do believe the school secretary phoned at least twice.'

Robbie looked at his mother. 'I ... I've been out,' she said, glancing sideways at Emma, not wanting to upset her by saying she was the reason she'd been scouring the streets.

'Have you any idea where he might be? I must say, it's rather odd, as I know he couldn't wait for today.'

Vanessa wanted to shout, 'Would we be standing here like this, you fucking moron, if we had known he wasn't here?' Instead, she just said, 'OK, thank you.'

Not knowing what else to say, she turned away and the others followed her. It wasn't until they were at the school gates that she wailed, 'Well, talk about feeling crap... Where the hell is the little shit?'

'Come on, let's get home and we'll figure out what to do. Perhaps he got a really bad case of nerves, and he's hiding somewhere,' Sandra said, leading the way.

'I'll kill him, missing a chance like that. They don't come that often, the bloody idiot.' Robbie took hold of Suzy's hand, while Emma frowned all the way home, knowing her thunder had well and truly been stolen.

CHAPTER FORTY-FOUR

Lorraine ended the call, and told the taxi driver to drop her off at Houghton le Spring. Instead of going to her mother's, she'd arranged to meet her in the café. As she got out of the taxi, she could see her mother and her side-kick were already in there. From the way Peggy was waving her arms around, she was obviously holding court, and regaling the people on the next table with her tales.

Thank God they're laughing, Lorraine thought. With Peggy, it could go either way once she was on her soapbox and had a captive audience.

'Hello, love.' Mavis rose and kissed Lorraine's cheek. 'Got you a can.'

Lorraine smiled, pulled a chair out and sat down. She smiled and nodded at the couple on the next table, then turned to Mavis. 'I need you to go back to the hospital to sit with Luke, Mam–'

'How is he?' Peggy interrupted.

'Much better.'

'Well, that's a godsend...' She turned to the couple who were taking the chance to escape, and were rising from their seats. 'He's a copper, you know. My god-daughter's lover, the one I told you about, the one in hospital.'

'Peggy!'

'What? I'm only saying, like.'

Lorraine shook her head. 'I want the pair of you to sort of stand guard, 'cause I have a sneaky feeling that the minute my back's turned, he'll be off trying to straighten this mess out himself, and Fyfe would just love that.'

'No bother, love,' Mavis replied.

'OK, get a taxi.' She pulled a twenty pound note out of her purse.

'Eee, no pet, you keep your money. We can afford a taxi, can't we, Mave?'

'Peggy, take it.' Lorraine demanded.

'Well, if you put it like that...' Peggy snatched the note, while Mavis tried not to smile, knowing that Peggy would have taken the money all along.

'So should we take him some more grapes in?' Mavis asked.

'He hasn't eaten the first lot yet, nor the five or six other lots that people have brought in throughout the day.'

'By "people", you mean coppers?' Peggy grinned.

'Is there any way to control that gob of yours?'

'No.'

'OK, I'm off. Got to get to the station. Don't forget, Mam, he is not to leave that room, whatever he says.'

'Oh, under room arrest.' Peggy looked wide-eyed at Mavis. 'You know what that means? Me and you are coppers!'

'Get her out of my sight.'

'Come on, Peggy, let's go.' Laughing, Mavis took hold of her friend's arm. 'Bye, love.'

'Bye.' Lorraine blew her mother a kiss.

'See you pet. And don't you worry, we'll look after the gorgeous hunk for you.' Peggy grinned at Lorraine.

Lorraine waved as they went out the door. She picked her can up and took a sip, then the smell of roast beef coming from the table next to her made her realise just how hungry she was. The station could wait ten minutes or so. She needed to eat. She ordered a chicken sandwich and a Bakewell tart, and enjoyed them both. Then, looking along the street out of the large window, she noticed the street lights starting to come on.

She saw the police tape cordoning the shop off and decided to walk along.

The constable standing with his hands behind his back outside of the shop turned out to be Carter. Lorraine was surprised. Carter could be put to better use elsewhere.

'What are you doing here?' she asked, on reaching him.

'DI Fyfe, boss.'

'What? Who gave her the right?' she said, thinking, the cheeky sod, she's done this on flaming purpose to get Carter away from the station, in case he finds out anything and passes it on to me.

Well, the bitch has picked just the right time to start a war.

'As far as I know, boss, Clark said you had enough on your plate with Luke the way he is, and that she was in charge of this case an' all.'

'Did he now.'

'Aye, boss. Well, DI Fyfe said that he did. Say that she was in charge, that is.'

'Hmm. Best I get down to the station and sort this little misunderstanding out, then.'

Carter grinned. 'Yes, boss. Thanks, boss.'

As she hurried down to the police station, Lorraine was foaming. 'How dare she?' she muttered as she passed Barclays Bank. 'The cheeky cow.'

Walking briskly, she threw a smile or a nod at people she knew as she passed them, although the smile was more of a grimace.

Because her mind was mostly on Luke, she didn't see the tall man, standing outside the recently closed down video shop across the road, watching her. Nor did she see him cross the street, heading in the same direction as her.

CHAPTER FORTY-FIVE

Sandra used her key to open the door. Usually it was quite stiff, but somehow this once it opened smoothly.

She walked down the hallway to the kitchen. She needed coffee, and time to think. 'Where the hell have you got yourself to, Darren?' she muttered, picking the kettle up from its stand and moving to the sink to fill it up.

I reckon he lost his nerve.

Poor kid.

And as usual Vanessa's over-reacting, wanting to call the coppers on a fifteen year old 'cause he didn't turn up for school. Especially as it's hardly four o'clock.

Four o'clock!

Not much time to sort out what I'm going to sell before tomorrow. Thank God Vanessa had thrown her a lifeline. Why the hell she hadn't thought of it herself, she didn't know.

Though if she was honest, she probably had for a fleeting moment, only she treasured her stuff.

That's all it is, stuff.

What to sell though?

She looked around as if the answer to her questions would suddenly appear on the walls. Sighing, she glanced down at her rings. No, she could never do that.

It's a way out.

It's just a quick fix.

'It'll get the bastards off me back, though,' she muttered, looking again at her wedding ring and engagement ring. 'I could always say they slipped off and fell down the plughole, he'd be none the wiser.'

She argued with herself over and over as she wiped the benches down. Then she remembered her grandmother's ruby ring. Her heart fluttered with excitement.

How the friggin' hell could I have forgotten that? She breathed deeply, unable to keep the smile off her face. The ring should pay all of the debt and leave some over.

Now, where is it?

The last time she remembered seeing the ring was at least five years ago, when one of her Christmas presents from her eldest had been a new jewellery box.

Suddenly it came to her.

'Bottom drawer. It's in the bottom drawer.

Get in! Problem solved.' She almost ran up the stairs.

She was so intent on digging the jewellery box out of the drawer, she never head the bedroom door close, nor the passage of footsteps across the thickly carpeted floor. She screamed loudly a moment later, when a hand clamped her shoulder and squeezed.

CHAPTER FORTY-SIX

After a meeting with Clark, in which Lorraine assured him that she was perfectly capable of keeping her mind on her job, especially now that Luke was on the mend and out of danger, he reinstated her – much to Fyfe's dismay. Smiling at Fyfe, who threw a scowl her way, she left Clark's office and headed for her own as Fyfe and Clark left for home.

A few minutes later, she was questioning Dinwall who, with Sanderson, had made record time down from Scotland. 'So, run it past me again. How ... why do you think it's the brother, Dinwall?'

Dinwall, like Sanderson, had taken ten minutes to shower and shave. He now wore grey slacks with a red jumper over a grey shirt. He scratched his chin. 'Dunno, boss, one of them things. He seemed to be a bundle of nerves, very volatile.'

Lorraine looked at Sanderson. He shrugged. 'He's right about the way the brother acted, boss, but I wouldn't like to swear to it being him.'

'OK. As soon as they get him down here, I don't care what time it is, phone me. Now here's what I've been thinking. It's a serial killer all right, one that has freedom to roam, a job that takes him around England, and on a couple of occasions France and Germany. My guess he's either a rep for a global company or a long distance lorry driver. Which leaves the brother out – according to the report on him, he works in the family farm shop.'

'How do you figure that, boss?' Sanderson asked.

Lorraine walked over to the board, where she had pinned up some new pictures. 'In 2011, Katja Schultz was found at the side of a road. It looked as if she'd been thrown from a moving vehicle. She'd been stabbed in the back, and, her whole left leg was missing, hacked off at the thigh.'

'The bastard,' Dinwall muttered, staring at the girl's picture. 'Pretty thing, an' all.' He glanced over the board, at half a dozen pictures of different girls. 'They're all blondes,' he suddenly blurted out.

'Yes. And all of them with missing parts,'

208

Lorraine said.

'Except for one part.' Sanderson walked over to the board and pointed to each individual picture in turn. 'They all have their heads.'

'He's making his very own ideal woman,' Dinwall gasped.

'Yes,' Lorraine agreed. 'What got me thinking was when he tried to hack off the wrong hand, he must have realised, and went for the other. A trophy taker wouldn't have been too bothered which part he actually had, as long as he had a piece of each kill for his cabinet. In fact, they mostly go for the same part on each victim.'

'So, judging by the emerging pattern, he still hasn't found the face of his ideal woman,' Sanderson said. 'No wonder this has been kept quiet.'

'He's still looking,' Dinwall muttered.

'Hmm.' Lorraine frowned at Dinwall. 'You still sure it's the brother?'

He shrugged.

'OK, get his passport checked, just so we can clear up if he was out of the country on any of those dates.'

'Sure, boss.'

CHAPTER FORTY-SEVEN

Martin had run all the way home, terrified in case they caught up with him. He could take no more. Mrs Archer had been the last straw. If that woman was back in Houghton, and teamed up with Dev, then God help anyone who crossed their paths. Pleased that his mother wasn't in, he rummaged in her medical cabinet. His grasping hand clasped around a bottle of pills. Drawing it out, he looked at the label on the bottle. Paracetamol. It looked like there was at least thirty in the bottle. That should do it.

Shoving the bottle in his pocket, he opened the back door and looked around. He wanted no one to see which way he was heading. He never wanted to be found, ever.

Closing the door behind him, he moved, head down, up Daffodil Close and slipped into the field where the new football ground had been built. From there he walked up to Newbottle, an invisible person. No one who passed him in car or on foot could see his face. No one knew that the boy they passed had been totally bullied into submission until he could take no more.

No one could see the haunted, terrified look in his eyes.

He walked up to Grasswell garage, called in for a bottle of water, then crossed the road.

CHAPTER FORTY-EIGHT

Sandra screamed. Her heart pounded hard enough to burst out of her chest. Terrified, she still found the courage to turn around. If she was going to die, she would look her killer in the eye.

She took one look at the man who was leaning over her, and collapsed in a heap on the floor.

'What the fuck, you idiot?' she yelled a moment later, as her husband grabbed her and gave her a cuddle.

She could feel his body shaking with suppressed laughter as he said into the warmth of her neck, 'Sorry, my love, really couldn't resist it.'

'I thought–'

'I was a burglar, rapist?'

'Something like that.'

'Since when did one of them wash the dishes first?'

She realised she hadn't checked the

kitchen. Good job, 'cause that would have spooked her, coming in to find the sink full of clean dishes when she was supposed to be home alone.

And that's why the friggin' key turned so easily. It wasn't locked.

Oh shit. Those twats will be back in the morning, and he'll be here.

What should I do? Her heart was racing nearly as fast as it had been before.

I should tell him.

He'll go crazy.

Shit ... shit ... shit.

'What's the matter? It wasn't that big of a fright. Was it? I'm sorry, I didn't think it would scare you like that.' He stroked her face. 'Honestly, I am sorry.'

Sandra sighed. 'I know, but seriously, think about it. I'm supposed to be here by myself. Wouldn't you get a shock?'

'You're right. Stupid thing to do. I feel crap now.'

'Anyhow.' Sandra pushed his arms away and stood up. 'What are you doing home in the middle of the week, eh? It's not like you. Really can't remember the last time you were home in the middle of the week.'

He stood and, towering over Sandra, said, 'The friggin' truck broke down again. That's the third time this year. Got the train down from Berwick, and seeing as all the other trucks are on the road, and mine's gonna take a few days to get mended, the boss said to have a few days off on him. So I thought I'd surprise you... Er, sorry again.'

Sandra sighed. 'OK. Let's go downstairs.' She glanced out the window before she left the room, pleased to see the street practically deserted.

She followed her husband down the stairs. As she looked at his broad back, she wondered again whether to tell him. It would create hell, but at least it would be over and done with.

But what if they don't come back until later tomorrow, and I can get him out of the house on some excuse or another? Then at least I'll have the chance to sell something and pay them off without him knowing.

Downstairs, he picked the TV remote up and flopped in front of the telly, while Sandra went into the kitchen to see what she could make for tea.

'Shit,' she muttered a moment later. 'There's frig all in. I'm just popping over the shop,' she shouted through. 'But first–'

Then she remembered that she hadn't told him about Darren being missing.

'So,' she said a few minutes later, when she'd told him everything she knew, and suspected, which was that Darren had basically chickened out. 'I'll just go and see if he's turned up yet, then I'll go get us some fish and chips, OK?'

'Fine,' he grunted, his eyes on the snooker final.

'Nice,' she muttered, as she shrugged her black coat on. It was warmer than the red one, and had a nice fur collar that she loved. Picking her purse up, she shoved it in her pocket after checking that she did have enough for fish and chips, seeing as the price for a good fish had rocketed lately. Going out the back door, she followed a single youth up the street, never guessing that it was Martin Raynor.

CHAPTER FORTY-NINE

'What the fuck's going on here, like?' Dev said, grinning, as they entered the Seahills through Tulip Crescent and saw the police car outside of the Lumsdon house.

Stevie pulled a face. 'Like you have no idea.'

Dev grinned. 'And so it begins.' For a long moment, he stared at the windows of the house as if picturing the inhabitants, and what they would be doing now that one of their number was missing.

'So what do we do now?' Stevie said, not liking the look on Dev's face. ''Cause you can guarantee that ginger cow will be out stomping about in them stupid boots, with the others. Safety in numbers, and all that crap, and there'll be no time for her to get money. 'Cause this lot will all get together and go looking. Bettcha anything you like.'

'Chill... Just play it cool, like we don't know anything that's going on. And paper isn't the only currency.'

'OK. Whatever.' Stevie frowned, not quite grasping what he meant by that.

They walked slowly along the street. Suddenly, Dev stopped. 'I want to see her.'

'You sure? But you said you didn't–'

'I want to see her. I want to see the horrible fucking bitch. I want to look her in the eye. I want to know why... And I want her to know everything, every little detail.'

Dev fell quiet, and Stevie did his best to bring him back to the plan. 'Thought we was looking for Fartin'?'

'Fuck him.'

'But your plan–'

'It'll still work.'

Stevie didn't want to agitate Dev any more than he already had. He'd seen what happened when Dev got agitated, more than once. How he'd ever made it out of prison was the eighth wonder of the world. Some nutty social worker with a degree in stupidity, who thought they could change the world.

'OK. They'll probably all come pouring out of the house shortly, like a bunch of fucking ants.'

Dev pulled out the makings of a rollie from his pocket. Leaning against Mr Skillings' wall, he made a joint. He was disturbed a moment later by the tapping of a cane.

Looking up, he saw Mr Skillings coming up his path towards him. Reaching his gate, Mr Skillings opened it, paused for a moment leaning on his stick, and looked right at Dev, who was only six inches away from the gate.

'What you looking at, old man?' Dev sneered.

'Don't think there's a name for it. Or if there was, it's dropped off.' Mr Skillings closed his gate behind him. 'And please take your filth away from my door.' Mr Skillings waved his hand in the air, dispelling the smoke as Dev lit up.

'Cocky old git.' Dev straightened up from the wall.

'You really don't want to find out just how cocky I am, so I suggest you leave. Now.'

For a brief moment, Dev was in awe. Thieves, rapists, bullies and hardened gangsters steered clear of him. He'd walked the corridors of Her Majesty's prisons with no fear. What he didn't know was that Mr Skillings had stood on the front line in more than one country, facing hundreds of men willing to kill him on an order. On each Remembrance Day, he wore a chestful of medals with pride. Although weakened physically by the passing of time, Mr Skillings still had nerves of steel, and the grit to stand up for what he believed in.

He looked at Stevie who, knowing some of Mr Skillings' history, at once dropped his gaze.

Dev, who missed nothing, weighed the old man up. He figured that, yes, he could take him down, probably dead easy, but he would suffer for it. The cane itself was a weapon. No, this guy, as old as he is, will have to be taken by surprise. And he will be, one dark fucking night.

Turning, Dev motioned with his head for Stevie to follow him. They went down through the cut between the houses and onto the deserted playing field, where Dev proceeded to smash the first swing he came to. Having just tested one of the goodies out of his bag, a giggling Stevie joined him.

Dev, however, was not laughing. In a white-hot rage, he systematically set out to wreak havoc on anything in his path.

CHAPTER FIFTY

DI Alison Fyfe strolled into the room as if she owned it. She looked around, took in the board with the photographs on, then turning to Lorraine said, 'Your boyfriend? He's off the hook.'

Lorraine looked at her. She thought Fyfe had gone home. If she's back, then something's turned up. 'My boyfriend has a name, and as a serving police officer in the borough, he deserves your respect. Also, if you would care to know, he's on the mend.' Lorraine scowled at her, but inside her heart was singing.

'As if he ever was on the hook,' Sanderson said.

'You know we had to do this by the book, seeing as the murder weapon did belong to him.'

'Yeah, yeah.' Lorraine turned away from her and began tapping her nails on her desk.

Fyfe bristled and glared at Lorraine with narrowed eyes. Spinning round on her red high heeled shoes, she started to walk out of the room. As she reached the door, Lorraine said, 'So – just how is he off the hook? You, er ... forgot to say.'

'The car was found at Finchale Abbey. So far, no DNA other than that belonging to DS Luke Daniels. We are still looking, but the sheer distance, given DS Daniels' state of health, makes it practically impossible for him to be the perp. So we have decided to go down a different avenue.'

'Well, thank you.'

Carefully, Fyfe closed the door behind her.

'She was dying to slam it,' Dinwall grinned.

'Proud of you, Lorry, you fairly kept your cool.' Sanderson patted her arm.

'Have youse any idea how fucking hard it was? She is the most aggravating person I've ever met.' Lorraine stood up and stretched the kinks out of her back. 'The sooner she's back in Newcastle, the better... Guess I'll get back to the hospital.' She glanced over at the board and shook her head. 'No leads at all, no reason. Or is there?'

'Too much evil in this world,' Sanderson said.

Lorraine sighed. 'How are people like this not picked up on early, so they can be sorted, and not left to ruin lives? There is no justification in this, none at all, whatever sort of life the bastard has led. Just who the fuck is he?'

'We'll get him.' Dinwall nodded his head.

Lorraine traced her fingers over the arm of one of the dead girls. In each picture, the

219

dead girl wore red and was draped provocatively. 'Why is this guy so special? Not one mistake to lead us to him, no DNA, no nothing.'

'That might be it, boss. Perhaps he's far from special. Not even ordinary, or so downright ugly that he has to make his own woman, because no others will even look at him,' Dinwall said.

'You've got a point.' Sanderson looked at Lorraine.

'OK. Here's what we do. Dwell on it, and in the morning I want your best ideas.'

The door opened, and Carter came in. 'Oh, boss, am I pleased to see you!'

'Feet hurting, lad?' Sanderson said.

'Aye. And that bloody cat? Somehow it got back into the shop. It's parading back and forth in the window, and no one left a key.'

'Oh dear. I thought the RSPCA would have come by now.'

'They did, but the stupid cat escaped out the back. They did hang around for a bit, but couldn't wait forever.'

Lorraine moved to her desk. Opening the drawer, she took out a set of keys. 'Here. Phone the RSPCA to come and get the poor thing. Take someone with you, and put them in the back yard till they get there. If it escapes again, it's you I'll be looking for, Carter.'

She had barely finished speaking when her

phone rang. Picking the receiver up she said. 'Hello?'

A minute later, she put the phone back on the hook. 'No good hanging around for the brother. According to Galashiels police, no one has seen him since youse guys were at the house.'

'That's it, then,' Dinwall said. 'Guilty.'

'Not necessarily. What about the other women? He might think he had a reason, however twisted, to kill his sister. But the others? It doesn't add up. No, I guess he's got something else to hide.'

'Hmm. None of it makes sense, does it?' Sanderson scratched his chin.

'Shit.' Dinwall shrugged his jacket on. 'Guess that's it. Pizza, and the thinking cap on.'

'I'd best get back to the shop then. Er ... is L–'

Lorraine cut Carter off. 'He's fine, Carter. Wouldn't surprise me if he's back to work in a couple of days.'

'Wow. Superman!'

Lorraine looked away to hide her smile, catching Dinwall's eye in the process, quite confident that she had won her bet.

CHAPTER FIFTY-ONE

'I told you it was a waste of time to call the coppers, Mam. Our Darren's not a toddler, and they think you're panicking because of what happened to our Claire,' Kerry said.

'I fucking well am, for God's sake. Anybody would.' She looked at Kerry. 'Have you realised just how lucky we were to get her back in one piece? I still have nightmares about it. I wake up screaming, I see her dead on a slab...Worse, I see her in some dirty shit-hole of a foreign place where her life isn't her own... She looks so sad in my dreams, Kerry.'

'It didn't happen, Mam.' Kerry took her mother's hand. 'It didn't happen, she's safe here with us.'

'But something's happened to our Darren. Something bad. I know it, you know it...' She spread her arm in a circle. 'We all know it. Today, of all days, for him to go walkabout? No way. He wouldn't do it. He was so happy this morning.' She looked over at Robbie, her eyes pleading with him to understand.

Robbie got up from the settee. 'Well, the best thing we can do is start looking ourselves. At the end of the day, the copper was

right. They can't go looking for every teenager that's missing at five o'clock in the
afternoon. But we can. Mind you, he's
getting a clout when I find him.'

'At least they've passed his details on, and
if any coppers see him, they'll pull him up.
That's something, I suppose,' Claire said on
her way in from the kitchen. Inside, she was
actually a lot more worried than she let on
to the others. She, out of them all, knew just
how easy it was for a gullible kid to be led
astray.

But Darren has his head screwed on, he
wouldn't do anything stupid, not to spoil his
chances, no way ... which really made it all
the more frightening. She looked over at her
mother's distraught face.

Oh God, this is what it must have been
like last year, when I did do something
stupid.

Filled with remorse, she walked over and
put her arm across her mother's shoulder.
'Sorry, Mam,' she whispered in her ear.

Understanding what she meant, Vanessa
patted Claire's hand. 'It's all right, pet. Would
you get those hot dogs out for the kids,
please? Best get everybody fed, actually.'

'Sure thing.' Claire went into the kitchen.
Taking a large tin of hotdogs out of the
cupboard, she opened them, poured them
into the pan, and started chopping onions.
Darren loved hot dogs with lashings of

onions and tomato sauce and these were supposed to be a treat for him, a sort of celebration, because no one had had any doubt that he would be picked up today. Even the football coach had been excited.

As she chopped the onions, she remembered what he'd said last night, what he was going to buy everyone when he was rich and famous. A new house for Mam had been top of the list, over on one of the posh estates. Only she hadn't wanted one, saying the last thing she would ever do was move away from the Seahills. Laughing, they had made plans to buy this house and the one next door and make it into a mansion, with a car for everyone parked outside.

Running her hands under the cold water tap, she dabbed at the tears with the back of her wrists, knowing that they weren't all brought on by the onions.

After a few minutes she said loudly, so her voice would carry into the sitting room, 'It's nearly ready for eating, Mam. Where's the brats?'

Vanessa looked up at Claire, giving her a puzzled frown. Quickly, she swung her head to Robbie.

'It's all right, Mam. They're just out playing with Melanie. You're worrying too much. When I get my hands on our Darren, I'll strangle the little shit. Bet you owt you like he's lost his bottle. Anybody looked under his bed? He's probs hiding there while we're going nuts.'

Vanessa shook her head in frustration. 'When was the last time you saw the girls?'

'Ten minutes ago, when they were out the front giving that copper grief.'

Vanessa settled back in her chair. 'Still, best call them in, eh? I'm not too keen on them hanging about outside when there's a murderer on the loose.'

'OK, whatever.' Robbie gave Kerry a sideways nod, and she followed him into the yard.

'What the fuck are we gonna do?' he said, closing the back door behind Kerry.

'I don't know. Wherever the little sod is, he wants to get his act together and get home, 'cause there'll be a queue waiting to strangle the twat.'

Robbie sat on the wall leading to the small vegetable patch that Vanessa had started a few months ago. Winter cabbages were in abundance, and those in the family who had never liked cabbage had soon learned that they now did.

He blinked when the street lights came on. He hadn't realised just how dark it was starting to get. He felt a sudden rush of worry. 'Do you think there's a chance something serious might have happened to him?'

'Do you?'

'I asked first.'

Kerry sighed. 'How many times can something like this happen to one family?'

'How many secrets can one mother have?' he retorted quickly.

Kerry froze as her brain replayed what he had just said. They had all had a huge shock last year when Claire had gone missing, and she found out something that had been hidden from her, something she had pushed firmly to the back of her mind. Something that was painful even now, after more than a year. And now, when things seemed to be getting good? She shivered, and looked sideways at her brother. The past was a place she never should have visited, and the last thing she wanted was another trip there.

CHAPTER FIFTY-TWO

'What do you want to go back up there for?' Stevie asked.

It was the last place he wanted to be. He'd thought of a way to get out of this mess – he just needed five minutes away from Dev to make a phone call. It looked like Fartin' had already opted out, and secretly Stevie didn't blame him. He needed to tell the coppers whose fault it was, before Fartin' lost it and grassed them all up. And the last thing he'd expected was to find Mrs Archer in the mix.

Could things get any worse?

So far I'm involved with murder, kidnapping and God only knows what else, none of it my idea.

OK, so I'm not lily white. I'm a bully. A thief. And a fucking coward!

The last thought had been hard to admit, though he knew it to be true. For a long time Stevie had not liked himself, but he was caught in the dog eat dog spiral, and getting out was practically impossible.

I've been bad, done bad things, some I haven't wanted to. But this? Man, I have to get away.

'Hey!' Dev shouted in Stevie's ear. 'What the fuck? You getting cold feet, eh, you bastard?'

Stevie jumped. Blinking hard, he said. 'No … no.' Shit, let me fucking guard down there, all right. 'No, just thinking about lying on a beach somewhere … with a nice curvy blonde.'

'Fat chance,' Dev laughed.

Stevie gave him a twisted grin.

'Come on, you perve.' Dev nudged Stevie in the ribs.

'Yeah. Why not.'

They headed up towards Houghton town centre and the Blue Lion.

CHAPTER FIFTY-THREE

Behind the car park facing the sports centre, hidden away amongst the trees, the forgotten cottage had lain deserted for over a hundred years. Overgrown by weeds, and with broken windows, the cottage was only remembered when locals got together and relived their childhoods.

Emma, Melanie and Suzy were skipping in the paths their parents, grandparents and those before them had skipped.

'We're not supposed to go in there,' Suzy whispered as the shadows lengthened. 'Our Robbie says there's ghosts in there. And they'll follow us home.'

Emma shrugged. 'I'm not frightened, soft sissy girl. How 'bout you, Melanie?'

'No, but we didn't get past the door the last time.'

'Well, this time we will. 'Cause there's no such things as ghosts, they're just fig ... fig...' She hesitated a moment, searching for the right word, which didn't come. Sighing with frustration, she went on, 'Whatever. So Mr Foster says, anyhow. Something about 'em, you know.' The other two gave her blank looks. After a moment she yelled, 'I know! Imagination.'

'Come on, then.' Pretending to be brave, Melanie moved forward, even though she was getting tingles of fright.

'But it's getting dark,' Suzy said, creeping behind them.

'Tut tut.' Emma looked crossly at her sister. 'Baby. Go home!' she hissed.

Suzy stubbornly shook her head. She'd rather follow them than go home by herself, because by the time she got out of the trees and into the Burnside, and ran all the way home, it would be really dark.

They crept closer. It was then that the snow started. The clouds had been full to bursting all day. At first it was light, but the closer they got to the house, the heavier the snow seemed to get. Emma peered into one of the filth-encrusted windows, but there was very little to see. It was even darker inside than out.

'Try the door,' Melanie said.

'You.' Emma looked at her friend.

'Are youse going in?' Suzy asked. Neither of the other girls missed the terror in her voice. Emma jumped a moment later, when Suzy grabbed hold of her jacket.

Melanie started to giggle nervously. 'Should we?'

'That's what we came for.' Emma would never let on to the others just how terrified she really was. Slowly, with the other two imitating her every move, she began to walk along the front of the house until she reached the door.

Still giggling, Melanie watched as Emma put her hand on the handle. Suddenly, her giggling stopped as if it had been cut off with a sharp pair of scissors. The handle turned easily, and the door swung open with a loud groaning sound. Then silence fell. All three of them popped their heads round the door frame, but there was nothing to see. The darkness inside was complete.

A second later, all three girls screamed as the loud groaning sound came again – only this time, from the bowels of the house.

CHAPTER FIFTY-FOUR

He opened his eyes.

He moaned. The pain was worse than ever.

Where am I?

Who am I?

He closed his eyes.

A moment later, they flew open again.

A noise!

He gasped. Girls! He knew them, but their faces refused to come.

He groaned loudly, then heard screams which were loud at first, but then started to fade into the distance.

'Come back,' he sobbed. 'It's me. I'm here. Please come back.'

CHAPTER FIFTY-FIVE

'OK, Mam. Youse two can get off home now,' Lorraine said, walking into Luke's room.

'Thank God,' Luke said. 'The pair of them have fleeced me dry.' He threw his hand of cards on the bed.

'Oh, you're such a bad loser.' Peggy batted her eyelids at him, as she picked the cards up and put them in the box.

Mavis stood up and kissed her daughter's cheek. 'He's gonna be just fine. Strong as a bull, this one.' She patted Luke's arm. 'Come on, you.' She looked at Peggy, who showed no signs of getting up.

'Do we have to? Lorraine likes the odd hand of cards, don't you, love?'

'See you, Peggy.' Lorraine smiled at her.

'OK.' With a flounce, Peggy stood up and followed Mavis. At the door, she turned and blew Luke a kiss. Luke blew one back, and Peggy laughed her way into the corridor.

'Oh, please for God's sake don't encourage her. She'll be proposing to you next.'

231

Luke laughed, and patted the side of the bed. When Lorraine sat next to him, he said, 'Really, Lorry, I feel so much better I could come home tonight.'

'No way. Twelve more hours observation, the doc said.' She turned to his locker. 'There mustn't be one flaming grape left in Sunderland, 'cause they're all in here.'

Luke laughed. 'Yes, even Clark popped in with a bunch... So, anything turned up in either investigation?'

'Hmm. They're waiting for the DNA database to get back with the results, should be first thing in the morning. The other case?' She shook her head, then proceeded to tell him everything they had figured so far finishing with, 'One thing that struck me on the way here is that all of the dead girls were wearing something red, apart from the last one who was naked.'

Luke put his arm around Lorraine, and she laid her head on his shoulder. After a moment, he said, 'Tell me what the victims were wearing, and in what sequence.'

'Right. Number one was wearing a red coat. Number two, a red dress. Number three, bra and panties. Number four, a negligee, and number five, nothing.'

'I think number five was meant to be his perfect body, and he panicked, or got carried away and forgot himself. Nothing else makes much sense.'

'It also means that he'll kill again, because he has yet to take a head.' She couldn't suppress the shiver that ran up her spine. 'He could be anywhere. Even sitting across the road in the café having his tea.'

'Hmm. Have any body parts been found minus the actual body?'

'Not that I know of. But they would be so much easier to hide. An arm in one county, a leg in another.'

Luke looked slightly sickly picturing what Lorraine had just said, but went on, 'And there's nothing at all in any of the previous cases to identify him?'

Lorraine shook her head. 'One of the reasons it was never made public. They took the decision to keep it quiet rather than panic people.'

'Really, it's a blank wall.'

'Yes. No one knows where or when he'll strike again.'

'Hang on...' Just as he was about to speak, Luke started sneezing. Lorraine grabbed the box of tissues and shoved them in his hand. The sneezing bout was quickly followed by a coughing fit.

'Ha, and this is the guy who wanted to come home tonight? No chance, mate.'

Luke took a deep breath. 'See? All better now.'

'Yeah, keep on taking the pills, mate. So, what were you gonna say?'

Luke pulled a face at her. 'Has anyone traced his path?'

'DI Medley from Coventry traced the first three.' Lorraine took a file out of her bag. 'Well, his first kill, we think, was actually near Coventry. A place called Rugby, just off the M1. The next one, six months later, was in Derby – again, close to the M1. Then, after another six months, Chesterfield.'

'The second one had her arms missing, so why does he want separate hands?'

'Could be scarring on them, birthmark, anything. My guess is this guy's going for perfection.'

Suddenly Lorraine's phone rang, startling them both. She looked at the caller ID, then smiled at Luke. 'Selina. Do you want to take it?'

Nodding, he held out his hand. 'Hello, kiddo, you back yet? I thought you would have been in by now. Before you ask, I'm fine. Getting better by the minute.'

For a few minutes he was silent, then said, 'Never... OK. I'll tell her. Bye, love.' He ended the call, and looked at Lorraine. 'The bloody train's only been broken down for two hours! Something wrong with the engine. They're just transferring them now, so it's gonna be around an hour or so before they get in.'

'Why didn't she phone before?'

'She thought it would be sorted sooner.

She says she'll see you at home.'

Lorraine nodded. She liked Selina, and her boyfriend Mickey was funny without even knowing it.

'Good. Looking forward to seeing them... Anyhow, the way you're talking, there could be some murders we're missing. Is that what you're thinking?'

'Yes. He's also a traveller of sorts.'

'You mean like with a fairground?'

'Could be.'

'Oh. We had him down more as a rep, or a lorry driver. But those funfairs travel all over the country, as well.'

Luke shrugged. 'Any of them could be suspects.'

'Right. A break of sorts, let the grey matter rest. What's on the box? And not bloody football!'

CHAPTER FIFTY-SIX

Melanie, Emma, and Suzy were still screaming as they passed Stevie and Dev halfway up the Burnside.

'What the fuck's spooked them?' Stevie said, standing still and watching them until they were out of sight. He frowned as he turned back to face Dev.

'They're girls. It doesn't take much, for fuck's sake.'

'Do you think–'

'No,' Dev snapped. 'I know what you're gonna say. What's done is fucking done. Leave it.'

'But, really, he's your–'

Dev was at Stevie's side in an instant. Fists clenched, he shoved his face into Stevie's. 'I said fucking well leave it, and I mean it. Just once more. Try it on, and you're fucking wasted. I shoulda known better than to tell the likes of you, fucking bastard.'

'OK, OK.' Stevie backed away. 'I just thought.'

'Well, fucking don't. I'll do the thinking. Got it?'

Stevie nodded. He was too frightened to speak. Dev turned and strode on. Such was his anger that his feet pounded against the pavement, jarring all the bones in his body. Not that he felt it. Dev felt nothing. He hadn't for as long as he could remember. His very soul had been starved out of him. There was only one person to blame for that, and she was going to get just what she deserved.

CHAPTER FIFTY-SEVEN

Going down the deserted hospital stairs, Lorraine stretched and tried to get the kinks out of her neck. Luke had fallen into a deep sleep half way through a re-run of the previous day's *Emmerdale*, so Lorraine had decided to slip away. She'd kissed his cheek, and wrapped her silver charm bracelet around his fingers.

She got into her car. It had been a really long day, and a nice hot bath and bed sounded great, especially if Selina and Mickey were on time. A few words with them, then she would go on up. She yawned, and looked into her rear view mirror before reversing out. In a few minutes she was heading towards Houghton le Spring.

As she passed the spot in Houghton Cut where Luke's car had been used as a murder weapon, she shivered, as goose bumps ran up her spine.

Five minutes later, she was turning into the street where she now lived with Luke. Locking the car, she started up the path, and noticed Rosie's curtain twitch. Knowing the old woman would want to know how Luke was, she slowed down and gave Rosie a minute to get her door open.

Her prediction had been right. Rosie's first words when she got the door open were, 'How is he then, pet?'

'He's fine, Rosie. The hypothermia didn't get too big of a grip on him, and you know how fit he is. In fact, he's chomping at the bit to get home.'

Rosie sighed her relief. 'Well, that's great news... Don't you go and get him out of there before he's ready, mind you.'

'Not gonna happen, Rosie.'

'By the way, I have something for you.' She turned and disappeared into her house, leaving Lorraine frowning her puzzlement.

A minute later she was back, with a huge bouquet of pale pink lilies.

'For me?' Lorraine said, smiling her pleasure at Rosie.

Taking the flowers, Lorraine looked at the card. 'I LOVE YOU.'

'He must have got one of the nurses to go out for them. Or probably Mam, 'cause he had no money on him. Then again, only Peggy would forget to write his name on.'

Rosie nodded. 'He's a lovely lad you've got there.'

'I know. Thanks for taking them in, Rosie.'

'No bother, pet. Goodnight.'

'And you too, Rosie.' Lorraine made her way inside. She was expecting Selina and Mickey in half an hour, so she left the latch off. Closing the curtains, she didn't notice the blue van pull in and park at the end of the street.

She went upstairs and started to run the bath. She loved Luke's bathroom, all white tiles with pale blue and navy blue shiny squares randomly spotted here and there. Shaking out what was left of her favourite jasmine scented bubble bath, she threw the empty container into the small bin under the sink. With both taps running fast, she never heard the front door open. Stripping her clothes off, she slid into the bath, lay down until she was covered in bubbles, and closed her eyes.

CHAPTER FIFTY-EIGHT

'Right, Mam,' Jacko said, getting up from his seat. 'I'm just gonna see where the little scamp is.' He was wasting his breath. Doris was sound asleep.

Shrugging his brown leather jacket on, he quietly opened the door and stepped out into the dark. Melanie was already coming down the path.

'And where have you been? You know better than to be out in the dark.'

'We was only playing, Dad.' She looked at

him. A more perfect picture of dignified innocence could not be found.

'Yeah, right. Rules is rules, madam. No telly tonight.' He gave her a disapproving look.

'What?'

'You heard.'

'But it's not even six o'clock yet, Dad,' she wailed.

'It's still dark. Get in the house.'

In a huff, and mumbling to herself, Melanie walked past Jacko, who turned and followed her.

Kids, he thought, just how far do you go, to warn them of the dangers out there without frightening them for life.

Ten minutes later, sitting by the fire with her blue pyjamas on, Melanie was staring at her father as he read his newspaper. Suddenly he said, 'What, Melanie?'

Startled, Melanie said, 'How did—'

'I've got eyes in the back of me head. So what were you gonna say? If it's the telly on, no.'

'Dad...' She hesitated for a moment, then said quickly, 'Is there really such things as ghosts?'

Jacko put his newspaper down. 'Why do you ask that?'

She shrugged. 'Just wondered.'

'Did you, now? Seen one lately, have you?'

Melanie wondered if she dare tell him

240

about the haunted house. She was in trouble already, and it was nearly Christmas. She had done the usual pre-Christmas search, and come up with nothing.

What if I tell him about the haunted house, and he cancels Christmas?

Dad wouldn't do that.

He might.

Whatever! Nana wouldn't let him.

She decided she had to know.

'Dad, have you ever been to the haunted house? When you were a kid.'

Jacko stared at her. 'That's where you and the girls have been, isn't it.'

'Noooo.'

'Don't lie, Melanie.'

Melanie's face went red. She shuffled her feet for a moment and her bit her lip, before muttering. 'Sorry, Dad.'

Jacko tried to keep a straight face, but it was becoming hard to do so. 'Did you see a ghost?'

'No. But we heard one.'

'What?'

'Yeah. It made a groaning sound, so we ran away.'

He laughed out loud. 'You ran away, did you? Well, pet, I don't blame you, 'cause I would have ran as well. Maybe not as fast as my mate Len, but fast enough, believe me.'

'Did you and your friend go there?'

'Aye, but we never heard no groaning

sounds, and that's a fact. Len would have been off like a shot, with the rest of us not far behind him.'

Melanie stared at him for a moment, thinking it over, when Doris startled them both by laughing. 'Ain't no such things as ghosts, pet, so don't go worrying about them. There's more harm in the living than the dead.'

They all got a shock a moment later, when there was a loud banging on the door.

CHAPTER FIFTY-NINE

He opened his eyes again. The pain in his side had gone. Now everything felt numb.

The memory of the girls screaming came back.

I know who they are.

But why can't I remember them?

Why can't I see their faces?

He tried to move, managed a wriggle to the left, when whatever he'd been lying on moved with him and came crashing down, taking him with it.

The noise reverberated over and over. Then suddenly there was an overwhelming silence.

CHAPTER SIXTY

Selina and Mickey got out of the taxi, both of them lugging a wheeled suitcase behind them. They walked up to the house. As the sitting room light was on, Selina tried the door. It opened and, smiling, Selina walked in shouting Lorraine's name.

Selina would rather have gone straight to the hospital, but the last text she'd received from Lorraine had said that her father was out for the night, and that he was so much better, but still needed rest.

After a few minutes and a search into the kitchen, she gave Mickey a puzzled look.

'She might be in the shower,' Mickey said, as Selina took off her short denim jacket. The red dress she wore was low cut, and very short. Selina was a lovely dusky shade, the offspring of a black father and a white mother, with large brown eyes. A healthy glow enveloped her, and to look at her no one would believe that less than a year ago she'd been heavily addicted to drugs. Mickey grinned. He loved to see her in that dress, and couldn't get enough of looking at her. Mickey had grown unexpectedly taller than he thought he ever would have. His mass of unruly black curls was still exactly that.

'Can you hear the shower?'

Mickey shook his head. 'Bath?'

'Probs. Let's get something to eat.' Going into the kitchen, Selina opened the fridge door. 'Hmm, not much in here...' She looked around. 'Guess it's beans on toast, unless we get a takeaway.'

'That'll do me.'

'OK. You order a pizza, while I go and see if Lorraine is in the bath. I need to ask her how Dad is.'

Mickey took his mobile out, and was about to ring for a pizza when his mobile rang in his hand.

'Well, hello there, mate,' he said, checking the caller ID and seeing that it was his best friend Robbie. 'How you?'

A minute later, he said, 'I'm on my way.' Putting his mobile away, he went to the bottom of the stairs and shouted for Selina.

She appeared at the top of the stairs. 'She's not here.'

'What?'

'Lorraine, she's not here. She's not anywhere. I've searched every room. And the bath's full, still warm, in fact.'

'Maybes she had to go out fast. Something might have happened in our lovely little town. She is a copper, you know.' He grinned.

'You reckon?'

'Aye... But we've gotta get down to Robbie's. His brother Darren's gone missing and people are going out looking. We gotta help.'

'OK, I'll change this dress.'

'Need any help?'

'Not likely.'

Going into her bedroom, Selina changed into a pair of blue skinny jeans and a cream jumper. All the while, she was puzzling over the full bath and the empty house.

Mickey's probably right, she thought. Lorraine must have been called out. Still a bit odd, though. And I can't call Dad, 'cause he's got no phone.

Back downstairs, she took Mickey's hand and looked into his eyes. 'Are you sure we shouldn't tell anyone? 'Cause to me, it looks a bit fishy.'

'That's 'cause your dad's a copper, who lives with a copper. Anyhow, who would we tell? The coppers?'

'Very funny.'

Mickey laughed. 'Come on, we better get down to Robbie's, and hope Darren turns up before we have to go trekking in the flaming snow.'

'OK.' She looked at her denim jacket. It was wet just from their wait for the taxi. Shaking her head, she reached for her pink duffle coat.

'Well, one thing's for certain. We won't lose you.'

Selina slapped the back of his head. 'That's enough of your cheek. Come on. We've gotta get down to the Lumsdons' and help find that Darren.'

'Hope he's all right. Strange that he had a Sunderland scout coming the day he decides to go walkabout.'

CHAPTER SIXTY-ONE

There was a breeze coming from somewhere to the left of her. She could feel it on her bare skin. Had she fallen asleep and left the window open? Her hands felt restricted. She tried to move them, as pins and needles set in.

It was then she realised they were tied behind her back.

She took a deep breath, trying to calm herself.

She opened her eyes, but could see nothing. When she blinked, her lids kept touching something.

Then suddenly, whatever had been wrapped around her eyes was whisked away.

The first thing she saw was a red dress on a coat hanger that was hooked over a wardrobe door.

The first thing she heard was a deep male voice saying, 'I love you...'

CHAPTER SIXTY-TWO

Emma watched from the corner of the crowded room. Kerry had made tea for the dozen or so neighbours gathered there to help look for Darren, and not one of them had once said that they had seen her on TV.

It wasn't fair. Even Robbie had told her to be quiet when she'd asked him about ghosts. Kerry had laughed at her, and none of them were worried that Suzy wasn't hungry, and wasn't that a first?

It's all Darren, Darren, Darren.

Darren's football, weeks and weeks of it. Be careful you don't sprain an ankle when you run, can't have you missing this chance, you know.

Kerry's running, huh. Heard enough about that, an' all. Over and over... Madam Kerry... And now it turns out...

She pulled a face at Suzy in the opposite corner. The brat can sing – so what? None of them have been on the telly, like me.

And none of them can hear ghosts either. Well, maybes Suzy. And she couldn't even tell them about the ghosts 'cause she would only get wrong again. But not Suzy. It would all be my fault again. Not that they're interested, like.

Huh. They would be if Suzy had said.

She glared at her sister again. Watched as Robbie sat down beside her and gave her a cuddle.

I hate you all, she thought. Jumping up, she ran upstairs and flung herself onto her bed.

Selina and Mickey followed Jacko up the path. When they were all inside, Robbie thanked everyone for coming and suggested that they all pair off. Mr Skillings was to keep watch on the street, and anyone who saw or heard anything was to report back to him. Robbie had phoned the police and told them what they planned to do. Their answer had been yes, go ahead, we'll let the patrols know, and yes, we are still keeping an eye out for him.

Kerry had laughed at him. 'It's a fucking joke, man, its still pretty early and they think we're getting all het up about what they look at as a street kid who knows what he's doing.'

'Don't pretend you're not a bit worried, Kerry.'

'A bit, yes, I suppose, just because of the football. I don't think he would have missed it on purpose. But he wouldn't be in at this time anyhow, and all I know is, he's gonna feel a right prat when he finds out about all the fuss.'

'Better safe than sorry. I guess what happened to our Claire, and you, is gonna be with us forever. And I'm terrified one more shock just might push Mam over the edge.'

They both turned to look at Vanessa, who was walking round the room thanking everyone for coming to help.

'OK, time to go.' Robbie shouted up the stairs for Emma. She and Suzy were to go straight over and sit with Doris and Melanie.

Still in a huff with everyone, Emma flounced down the stairs and, without waiting for Suzy, marched over to Doris's house. Robbie shook his head as she passed him.

'Come on, Suzy, I'll see you over.'

A few minutes later, he and Jacko set off in the direction of the Burnside. Kerry had used the paper shop's copier to print off a few hundred pictures of Darren, and the whole search crew were armed with them.

CHAPTER SIXTY-THREE

Stevie and Dev watched as people left the house and drifted off in pairs.

Playing the part, Stevie sniggered. 'Like they know where to look. Fucking idiots.'

'Stupid bastards. Who's the new chick? The looker with that curly haired twat?'

'That's Selina, that black copper's kid.'

'Fuck off.'

'I kid you not.'

For a moment Dev was quiet as he stared at Selina.

'And that's Kerry and Claire?' He gestured with his head towards them as they passed. Stevie didn't miss the narrowing of his eyes.

'Yes. She does look like that bird on the...' Stevie was starting to feel nervous, wondering just what Dev was planning. Obviously he wasn't listening to him.

'And that's Emma and Suzy that just went into that house, with just the old wife inside to watch them, 'cause the bloke with the eye patch is out hunting.'

'Er, yes.'

'Interesting.'

'Er... she's not just any old wife, Doris.

She'll have a go, mind. Big bastard an' all, I wouldn't like to mess with her... Plus it looks like Mr Skillings is patrolling the street.'

'You're a right fucking fanny, ain't you?'

'Just saying.'

'Do you honestly think two old farts like them bother me?' Dev's voice rose with each word.

'No, no. Just saying, that's all.'

CHAPTER SIXTY-FOUR

Vanessa and Sandra walked down past the Beehive, towards Fencehouses.

'Did you find your aunt's ring, then?'

'Yes, but there's a problem. The hubby's back.'

'Shit.'

'Well and truly.'

'Excuse me.' Vanessa stopped a middle-aged man. 'Have you seen this boy today at all?' She held out a picture of Darren.

The man glanced briefly at the picture, shook his head and walked away.

'Huh. Ignorant git,' Vanessa said.

'There'll be some like that, always is.'

'So what you gonna do?'

Sandra knew that Vanessa needed to talk to keep her mind from going crazy with worry, but the problem was, she still didn't know exactly what she was going to do.

She was searching for an answer without having to lie to her friend because, with all the lies she'd already told her husband, she felt as if she was sinking in them.

Just then, two teenage girls walked round the corner. Vanessa pounced on them.

'You Darren's Mam, like?' the shorter of the two girls asked, looking from the picture to Vanessa.

'Yes. Have you seen him today?'

'No.' She shook her head and looked at her friend.

'Never seen him for ages.'

Vanessa sighed. 'Cheers, girls. Thanks.'

Beginning to wonder if this was a good idea, being out here in the freezing cold when most folks were in their homes beside the fire, especially if Vanessa was going to get her hopes built up every time they showed someone his picture, Sandra moved on. She looked across the fields to her right. The area was vast, with many hiding places, and she knew that, from further up the bank towards Newbottle on a clear day, you could see right up and past Consett.

God, the kid could be anywhere.

'Do you think we're ever gonna find him?' Vanessa asked, her voice low and full of worry.

'It's early days, love. He's probably just

chilling somewhere, feeling crap, if it's because he bottled it. He'll not want to face any of you.'

She didn't add that, although this was what most of them thought, in her eyes Darren was not the kind of kid to give up like that. And she guessed that Vanessa was thinking the same, and just going along with the idea, because that would mean that he most likely hadn't come to any harm.

They passed a few other people on their way. None had seen any sign of Darren.

Neither of them noticed that they were being followed.

CHAPTER SIXTY-FIVE

Lorraine froze. It was a deep, scratchy sort of voice, a voice she'd never heard before.

What the hell had happened? The last thing she remembered was being in the bath. And then it came to her. He had walked in, and before she'd had a chance to react, he had covered her mouth and nose with a cloth.

It must have had chloroform on it. She wrinkled her nose. There it was, just a faint hint.

She saw him step from behind her. In his

253

hand, he held a large knife. She could feel her heart banging against her ribs.

She was helpless.

CHAPTER SIXTY-SIX

Jacko and Robbie walked through the Burnside estate, handing leaflets out and talking to people much the same way as the other searchers. But no one, young or old, had seen Darren that day. When they reached the Miners' Hall, they met up with Len Jordan who was walking his dog, Meg.

'Heard what was going on, so I've looked behind there. Nowt to see, and Meg never heard anything.' He patted the dog's head. 'She's damn good at sniffing things out, is Meg.'

'Great. Thanks, Len.'

'Danny's riding round in the van with Adam as well.'

Robbie felt his heart swell. It was then he realised just how kind and helpful people could be. He wanted to grab Len and hug him, but knowing Len, he would probably freak right out.

'So,' Len went on, 'I've looked behind the Miners' Hall and the doctor's surgery.' He looked up the street. 'Still got the sports centre and that new health centre to do.'

'Good,' Jacko replied. 'We'll do down the allotments. Catch you in a bit.'

Len nodded, and moved towards the sports centre.

Jacko looked at Robbie. With a smile, he shrugged, and crossed the road towards the allotments. Following him, Robbie looked at the mass of trees behind the car park. As he switched his torch on, Jacko switched his on, and they headed into the dark track with houses on one side and allotments on the other.

Both of them played their torches over the first allotment, covering every shed and chicken run. 'No luck there,' Jacko muttered as they moved to the next one.

'Fuck off! Fucking kids,' a man shouted, nearly frightening the life out of Robbie.

'It's all right, Joe,' Jacko said. 'We're looking for a missing lad.'

'Oh, you shoulda said. Well, he's not here. No bairns allowed in here. Ain't seen any all day, thank God.'

'OK, Joe. You've got my number if you see him.'

'Aye, but me eyes ain't that good in the dark.'

'Bye.'

They moved on, flashing their torches every which way, startling a few cats, both of them thinking the same – that their task was

255

a hopeless one.

Robbie stopped to check his phone. He'd put Darren's picture up on Facebook, and although there were lots of 'Hope you find him', and plenty of shares, there wasn't one message saying someone had seen him.

With a sigh, he shoved it back in his pocket. Jacko frowned at him, and Robbie proceeded to tell him about the internet.

'Guess it's got its uses then. Our Melanie's getting one of them laptop things for Christmas. Wasn't sure about it, like, but she's gone on and on...'

'There are child locks and guards.'

'Good, you can show me then. We better be getting back up and see how Len's got on, 'cause there's nowt doing here.'

CHAPTER SIXTY-SEVEN

The blade looked brand new as it flashed under the light. He was standing in front of her, tilting his head from side to side as he stared at her. Lorraine stared back.

'I love you,' he said.

Lorraine had already guessed that it was him who had sent the flowers.

'Then if you love me, let me go.'

'Can't do that.'

'Why?'

'Because it would be silly. I've searched for years, all over the country. I knew one day I would find you. One time I nearly gave in. That was in Dundee, and I nearly settled for second best.'

Lorraine's heart sank. His voice kept changing from deep bass to an almost childish singsong tone. And, she realised, Dundee had not been on the list. Just how many girls in how many years has this bastard murdered?

She struggled with her hands. If she could only get her thumb free...

He must have noticed, because he moved slightly forward and stepped around her to check. Bastard, she thought, just come close enough, just a little closer. He smelt of garlic and days-old sweat, and it made her feel sick.

Facing her again, his face suddenly changed. 'Oh, please forgive me.'

Lorraine frowned, as he put the knife down and started to strip his clothes off.

CHAPTER SIXTY-EIGHT

Carter tried Lorraine's phone again. Still no answer.

'Wonder if I should go round hers?' he muttered.

Undecided, he sat down, picked the *Sunderland Echo* up, flicked through it, couldn't decide if there was nothing worth reading or if it was because he just couldn't get interested.

He looked at the clock and decided, seeing as there was at least an hour before he had to pick his mother up from the bingo at Washington, he would drive down to the Seahills and see if he could help in the search for the missing Lumsdon boy.

He wished he could phone Luke, but Luke had no phone. It had been good to pop in and see him today, and find him looking so well. And it had thrilled him that Luke looked so pleased to see him. Luke was one of the best men he knew.

And he was so beautiful.

He got that faint tingling feeling in his heart when he thought of Luke. Jumping up from his chair, he pushed the thought and the feeling to one side.

Stop it, he told himself. Luke is with Lorraine. Why the hell am I even thinking it could be otherwise?

Stupid!

He grabbed his car keys, shrugged into his jacket and headed out to his car.

CHAPTER SIXTY-NINE

Luke opened his eyes. Feeling something tugging on his hand, he looked down. A soft smile played on his lips when he saw Lorraine's charm bracelet wrapped around his fingers.

A nurse popped her head round the door. 'How are you?' she asked.

Luke had not seen this one before, a pretty redhead with green eyes. He realised while he'd slept there must have been a shift change. 'I'm good, really good. Could I make a phone call?'

'Don't see why not.'

'Can you reverse the charges on the phone?'

'Not sure, but you can try.'

'Cheers.' Luke got out of bed, put his dressing gown on and walked slowly to the door. Take it easy, he kept telling himself, don't want to give them any excuse to keep me in.

The truth was, though, that he really did feel good enough to get out of here. He took the lift to the downstairs reception where the phone was located, and rang Lorraine's number. No answer. Tutting, he put the phone down, and decided to go out for some fresh air.

Outside, there were four people huddled against the cold in the corner, smoking.

Luke nodded and smiled at them. One woman, a tall brunette, walked over. Blowing smoke out of her mouth, she said, 'So, what you in here for?'

'Sort of flu bout. You?'

'Appendicitis. Can't friggin' wait to get out, it's like a bloody jail sentence. Day after tomorrow, hopefully. I'm Marie, by the way.' She held out her hand.

'Luke.' He took her hand and shook it. 'I'm out of here tomorrow. Nice to meet you, too. Think I'll wander back in now. Trying to make a phone call.'

'OK.' She winked at him. 'See you around.'

Luke smiled, thinking, not if my Lorraine sees you first.

He tried Lorraine's mobile again. Still no answer. Frustrated, he looked at the phone, muttering 'Where the hell are you?'

Without knowing, he had echoed Lorraine's words of twenty four hours ago.

CHAPTER SEVENTY

Selina and Mickey crossed over the road from Grasswell garage, and walked up to the local tip underneath Table Rock. The entrance was well lit, and a man was sitting reading a newspaper. They were nearly at his station before he spotted them. Startled, he put his newspaper down.

Before he could speak, Selina handed him one of the flyers.

'Have you seen this kid knocking around today?'

Looking at them both suspiciously, he took the flyer, studied it for a moment, then shook his head. 'Not while I've been on duty. Mind you, I didn't start till six, so one of the daytime guys might have seen him.'

'OK, thanks.' Mickey said as they walked away.

Selina sighed. Looking at Mickey, she said, 'I think we've done just about everywhere up here, like.'

'Tell you what. We'll keep on this side of the road, and have a look through that batch of trees opposite the garage, then make our way down through Grasswell.'

She shrugged. 'Whatever, Mickey, but it's

getting friggin' colder by the minute. I wonder if that's why Lorraine's not in the house? What if they've found him, and it's not good news?'

Mickey put his arm over her shoulder. 'She might be still at the hospital.'

'No, I told you. Dad was asleep. She left ages ago. Don't you think its weird that the bath was still full, maybes we should tell somebody.'

'Like who?'

Selina shrugged.

'Well, not much we can do, about a bath full of water is there? Come on, let's get going.'

They walked over the grass to the tree line. 'It's fucking dark in there, Mickey.'

'We'll just weave in and out.' Stepping past the first few trees, Mickey ran his flashlight through the gaps in the trees. Slowly, they worked their way along, startling rabbit after rabbit. When they got near the end, Selina suddenly shouted, 'What's that?' She put her arm out, and stopped Mickey in his tracks.

'What? What?' he grunted. Selina had nearly winded him.

'Over there look. See, through that thick bunch of trees? There's something red.'

'I can't... Yes, there it is!' he yelled as their combined flash lights joined. 'Come on, it might be him.'

They ran through the trees, jumping here and there over roots, Mickey shouting Darren's name as loudly as he could.

When they reached what Selina had seen, it was to find a red hoodie, the arm lying over a tree stump.

Bending down, Mickey picked it up. 'Whose is this? Looks pretty new to me.'

Selina shrugged. 'I really don't know.' Turning, she flashed her torch around. A second later, she gasped. 'Oh, my God.'

'What?' Mickey jumped and spun round, the beam of his torch adding more light to Selina's.

'Is it Darren?' Selina asked.

'Shit, no... It's Martin Raynor.'

Quickly, they ran across the small clearing. Martin was lying face down on the ground, his still fingers touching an empty bottle of paracetamol.

Mickey covered him with his hoodie and tried to find a pulse, while Selina rang for an ambulance.

'They want to know how many he's taken,' she hissed at Mickey.

'How the hell would we know? Just tell them the bottle's empty.'

'OK.' She did so, then put her phone away. 'Mickey, is he still alive?'

'I think so.' He shrugged. 'I don't really know... But,' he lay down next to Martin and cuddled him, 'I read somewhere that body heat helps. Come here.'

Selina lay down on the other side of Martin. She put her arm over him, and moved in as close as she could. There were tears in her eyes as she said, 'I don't really know him, Mickey, but I hope he's gonna be all right.'

'He will be.' But Selina could tell by Mickey's voice that he was far from sure.

'Shouldn't we pick him up and keep walking him around? I've seen them do that on the telly.'

Mickey sighed. 'I really don't know.' Terrified now in case they were doing the wrong thing, he looked at Selina and shook his head. Together they cuddled Martin the best that they could, both of them praying they were doing the right thing.

'What's that?' Selina said a few minutes later.

'What?'

'Shh... It's the ambulance. I can hear it.'

'Fucking good lugs you've got.'

'Shh. Listen.'

Mickey's face lit up. 'It is! You go down to the road, and show them where we are. I'll keep him warm.'

A few minutes later, Selena was back with two ambulance men, one carrying a folded up stretcher and the other a medical bag. Quickly the man with the bag got to work, while Selina, Mickey, and the other medic looked on.

After what seemed like forever to Mickey and Selina, he looked up. 'He's still alive. Guess you found him just in time.'

'Is he gonna be all right?' Mickey asked.

'He's alive. That's what counts at the moment.'

Aware that the medic was really fobbing him off, Mickey sighed, picturing Martin on the first day of infant school, a shy kid who hid behind his mother at the gates and had to be practically dragged in by the teacher. They had after a few weeks become friends. Martin used to follow Mickey all over. Then, when they had moved to senior school and got put into different classes, Mickey had hardly seen him, only passing each other in the corridor now and then.

I did come over for you, Martin. I still wanted us to be friends. Why didn't you want to be my friend any more?

Mickey swallowed past the lump in his throat, and watched as the medics got Martin onto the stretcher. Quickly they got him down the small hill and safely into the waiting ambulance. Mickey gave the ambulance man Martin's name and address. The ambulance man in turn took their names, and complimented them both. A moment later, the ambulance drove off with all lights flashing and sirens screaming.

Selina put her arms around Mickey and,

assuring him that they had done everything they could, and that Martin was in the best of hands they headed for home.

CHAPTER SEVENTY-ONE

Lorraine stared at her captor, her heart pounding. Shirt off, he reached for his belt buckle.

Not this. Please, not this.

She looked at the clock on the wall behind his head. Eight fifteen. Would she live to see midnight?

She took a deep breath. Fuck the twat. If I'm going out, it's not gonna be quiet.

'OK, bastard,' she yelled. 'If you're gonna kill me, just fucking get it over with.'

CHAPTER SEVENTY-TWO

Noticing half a dozen people standing outside of the Miners' Hall, and guessing rightly that it was some of the search party, Carter pulled up.

'Any luck?' he asked.

'No,' Robbie said flatly.

'Oh.' Carter didn't want to upset them more by throwing statistics at them. He knew that roughly two hundred thousand people go missing in the UK each year, a good proportion being teenagers who have gone off in a huff, the majority of whom turn up the next day. He also knew that if someone didn't want to be found, it was a lot harder than anyone ever thought to find them, especially in the dark. He could even be watching them now, frightened to come out because of all the fuss.

'I'm sure he'll turn up. If he hasn't by midnight, phone the station again.'

'You reckon?' Robbie asked.

Carter nodded. 'I have to be somewhere, but I'll have a drive around first then I'll call back.'

'Sure. Thanks.'

They watched as Carter drove off, all of their spirits low. 'We gonna call it a night?' Len Jordan asked.

Robbie looked at Jacko. 'We've done just about everywhere we can think of.' The last thing he wanted to do was call the search off, but everyone by now was freezing – and to be honest, they weren't getting anywhere.

'It's like looking for a ghost, and the fog's coming down now,' Len said.

'What did you say?' Jacko asked.

'The fog's coming down.'

'No, before that.'

'It's like—'

'OK, got it.' Jacko turned to Robbie. 'Did the kids say anything about the haunted house when they came in?'

Robbie shook his head as he looked across the car park to the trees. 'Can't remember... Why?'

'Because they were there, and our Melanie said there were noises, so they ran away.'

'Do you think?'

'It's worth a look.'

Len nodded, and followed as Jacko and Robbie quickly crossed the road. Once they were through the car park and into the trees, Jacko and Robbie turned their torches on. Stepping off the path, they moved through the undergrowth until they came to the house.

'Brings back some memories all right,' Jacko said, playing his torch over the house.

'You never!' Robbie looked at him.

'Oh, we sure did.' Len smiled. 'Do you think it only became haunted when you was a kid?'

'Come on, then.' Jacko moved forward. The fact that he'd actually seen Len smile nearly freaked him out.

They got to the door, and Jacko reached for the handle. Slowly, with a groaning sound, the door opened.

CHAPTER SEVENTY-THREE

Vanessa and Sandra had run out of leaflets. Feeling really low, Vanessa sat down on the wall.

'What we gonna do, Sandra? I can't go on any more. Surely the coppers must realise by now that something really bad has happened to him.'

'I'll phone Kerry, see what's going on up there.'

A few minutes later, she put her phone down and, with a brief smile, said, 'Well, the coppers are finally taking it seriously. Kerry's out in a cop car with them. Seems that young copper, Carter? Called by and she jumped in his car. She said she's phoned you twice, and was just about to phone me.'

Vanessa took her phone out. 'Fuck. The battery's dead.'

'Does that bus go back up to the Seahills?' Dev asked, as a bus passed them.

'Aye.'

'Come on, then. You got any change on you?'

'Change? Exactly when was the last time you were on a fucking bus, like?'

Dev raised his eyebrows. 'A few years, as you well know, you prat. Well, actually, just yesterday.'

'Yeah, well. News flash. It takes a hell of a lot of fucking change to ride a bus these days.'

Dev pulled a five pound note out of his pocket. 'OK. When's the next one due?'

'Every twenty minutes or so.'

Looking across the road at Vanessa and Sandra, who couldn't really see them hiding behind the bus stop, outside the fish shop, Dev said, 'A hell of a lot can happen in twenty minutes or so.'

'What you planning?' Stevie's heart gave a jump. He did not like one little bit the way that Dev was staring at the two women, especially Vanessa.

But Dev ignored him. He was too busy thinking about his hands around her throat, and rehashing exactly what he was going to say to her.

CHAPTER SEVENTY-FOUR

He looked at Lorraine, disgust written on his face. Moving forward until he was standing in front of her, he stroked her cheek. Lorraine shivered at his touch. Revolted, she moved her head away, but he gripped her chin firmly and turned her head back to face him.

'How could you?'

Lorraine's eyes showed puzzlement.

'How could you, with such a beautiful face, talk with such a filthy mouth? YOU HAVE RUINED EVERYTHING!'

'Well, I'm fucking sorry about that.'

'Bitch.' He struck her hard across her face.

CHAPTER SEVENTY-FIVE

The three of them shone their torches inside the house. Slowly, Jacko stepped inside.

'I think this was a bad idea,' Len said from behind Robbie.

Jacko glanced back at him. 'Don't tell me you believe in ghosts.'

'Well, nobody really knows, do they? I mean, have you ever seen one? You should watch them ghost programmes on the telly, you'd get your eyes open then though... That's if you believe it,' he added quickly.

Barely stopping himself from punching Len in his eye, Jacko said, 'For God's sake, Len, just stand in the friggin' doorway and move the torch around.'

'OK.'

Robbie looked at Jacko, and couldn't help but grin. Shaking his head, Jacko moved forward. At first, there was very little to be seen. The place was hung with spiders' webs as if they were Christmas decorations. Something scurried along the far wall, and Jacko mouthed to Robbie, 'Rats.' Robbie shivered, but still stepped in until he was abreast with Jacko. Together they swung their torches from left to right.

Suddenly, Robbie was nearly knocked off his feet as Meg broke free from Len and bounded, barking her head off, into the middle of the room.

'Ow!' Robbie yelled as, losing his footing, he slipped and fell on his elbow.

The next moment, Meg disappeared. They all heard her yelp, then fall silent.

'Oh, what the– Meg!' Len shouted, moving into the house to stand next to Jacko, who was helping Robbie up from the floor. Together they pointed their torches at the spot where Meg had disappeared, exposing a huge hole in the floor.

'Meg!' Len shouted again, slowly stepping forward.

'Spread out,' Jacko said. 'Even the weight up, and tread careful, 'cause this floor looks like it could go at any minute.'

Being the lightest, Robbie, with Len hanging onto him at one side and Jacko the other, peered over the edge. 'Let go of me arm and grab me coat, Jacko, so I can use me torch.'

Jacko obliged, and the next moment Robbie was shining his torch down the hole.

'Yes!' he yelled. 'It's our Darren. He doesn't look too good, but it's him. He's there!'

'Yes!' Jacko echoed Robbie, as he reached for his phone.

'Meg?' Len asked, tensely.

'I can't... Hang on, there she is... Oh.'

'Oh what?'

'She's not moving.'

'What? Why isn't she moving?'

'Shit.' Jacko swung his torch around as he grabbed Len, to stop him reaching the hole in the floor. 'There must be a door. Step back carefully, Robbie.'

When he was sure that Robbie was safe enough, he played his torch over the wall on his left. 'There it is. Now, remember if the floor can give way under Darren, it will certainly give way under our weight.'

All three of them suppressed the urge to run out of the room. Very carefully, they made their way to the door. Once through, the door to the basement was facing them.

'Right, that looks like it. Or it could be that one there...' Jacko flashed his torch at another door further down the hallway.

Moving forward, Robbie opened the first door. It turned out to be an empty cupboard. They went to the next one, which had a stone staircase leading down. Practically running down the staircase, Robbie arrived at the bottom first. The door, however, was locked.

'Move back.' Jacko put all his strength behind his kick and the bottom of the door, many years old, shattered at once. Robbie used his shoulder on the top half, and the door folded in on itself. Pushing splintered wood out of their way, they all ran to the boy and the dog.

'Darren.' Robbie shook his brother's shoulder. 'Darren, it's me. Wake up, Darren.'

'Careful,' Jacko said. 'You don't know what damage he's done.' He looked at the ceiling. It was obvious from where Darren was lying that he'd fallen through.

'He's breathing, Jacko. He's fucking breathing.' Robbie's heart filled ready to burst, and his tears flowed freely as he looked up at Jacko.

Jacko squeezed Robbie's shoulder. 'Thank God.'

He looked at Len, praying that Meg was all right. Then he heard a whimper, and blew air out of his cheeks in relief.

'Aww, Meg,' Len said, gently patting the dog's side. 'I think she must have been stunned, there's blood on her head.'

A moment later, the dog howled in pain. 'Shit. I think she's broken her leg.'

'It's all right, Len. We'll get her sorted.'

Darren moaned, and tried to move.

'Don't, Darren. You're all right, the ambulance is on its way,' Robbie said.

Darren opened his eyes and stared at Robbie. 'Who are you?' He tried to shrink away from him, a terrified look in his eyes. 'Who are you?' he muttered again.

'It's me, Robbie. I'm your brother.'

'Brother?' He moved his eyes to Jacko and Len.

Both shook their heads and said together, 'Friends.'

'What happened, can you remember?' Robbie asked.

Slowly Darren shook his head. 'Can't remember nothing.'

CHAPTER SEVENTY-SIX

Cold and tired, Sandra and Vanessa had barely sat down on the bus when Sandra's phone rang. Before she had a chance to answer it Vanessa was back on her feet and handing out posters to the three other people on the bus, when she came back to her seat Sandra grinned at her. 'It's Robbie,' she said, looking at Vanessa with hope. Quickly she answered it, then screamed loudly, and laughed a second later.

'What?' Vanessa grabbed her arm.

'They've found him. The ambulance is there now.'

'Ambulance?' Vanessa's heart filled with dread. 'What? Why does he need an ambulance?'

'OK, yes, we'll come straight to the hospital.' She put her phone away. 'It seems he's fallen through the floor of the haunted house. Might have a broken arm, his memory's a bit dodgy, but he's alive, Vanessa.'

Vanessa put her head in her hands and burst out crying. As Sandra put her arm around her, neither of them saw the gloating look on the face of one of the men who had just sat down behind them.

CHAPTER SEVENTY-SEVEN

'You so disappoint me, with your potty mouth.'

'Tough.'

Glaring at her, he went to the corner of the room and picked up a music stand, which he placed in front of her. From a desk in the corner, he picked up a book of poetry and placed it on the music stand. He then switched on a tape recorder.

Lorraine looked from the book to the recorder and, guessing what he had in mind, said, 'Are you for fucking real, or what?'

'The longer you read, the longer you keep your tongue.'

'What?' she shouted.

'You see, you might have the perfect face for me, but I really can't have my perfect woman with such a dirty filthy mouth.'

Dear God. He's gonna kill again, take the tongue, and put it in my mouth. The realisation sent shivers up her spine. She gagged.

'Please don't be sick.'

'Fuck off.'

'See what I mean? Start reading … now.'

Lorraine looked at the book of poems. Fiction, she loved. Poetry, not so much. She flexed her hands, but the ropes were still as tight as they had been.

Where the fuck is the cavalry?

But she knew in her heart that the cavalry was never coming.

How can they?

And when they finally realise I'm missing, it will be too late.

'Read.' He pointed at page one.

Lorraine noticed the heavy nicotine stains on his fat fingers. The thoughts of those horrible hands touching her sent another shiver through her as she started to read.

DAY THREE

CHAPTER SEVENTY-EIGHT

Luke opened his eyes, stretched, yawned, and instantly realised where he was. He felt good, not even a sniffle hanging around, he thought, as he got out of bed. Sorting through the clothes that Lorraine had brought in, he went for jeans and a navy t-shirt, picked up a towel and made his way to the bathroom. He felt like singing. He was fine, and everything in his life was rosy. He would shower, shave and then phone Lorraine to come for him, or send somebody, anybody, even Dinwall, to pick him up.

The nurse caught him on the way back to his room. 'Looking good,' she said with a smile, following him into the room.

'Feeling good.'

'Well, the doctor says you still have to finish your course of antibiotics, so...' She handed him a pill.

'But–'

'Three pills today, three tomorrow. Paracetamol if the headache comes back. He'll be doing his rounds in an hour, and my guess is you'll be discharged.'

Reluctantly Luke took the pill, swallowed and put the glass of water back on the cabinet. 'An hour.'

'Tops.'

'I can do an hour. Just off to the phone.'

The nurse smiled, and her heart skipped a beat when he smiled back. She wondered again why the best ones were always taken.

Luke took the handful of change out of his pocket, that Lorraine must have slipped in without telling him, checked it over then fed the coin slot.

Five minutes later, he stared in puzzlement at the phone. Why isn't she answering? He tried his daughter, Selina, who picked up at once.

'Dad!' she practically shouted at the other end.

After a few minutes assuring her that he was fine, and no, there was no need to come in as he would be home shortly, and apologising for cutting her holiday short, he asked if she had seen Lorraine this morning.

For a moment there was silence. Then Selena said quickly, 'I ... we've never seen her, Dad. She ... er ... she didn't come home last night. We thought she might be working, or with you. I phoned her last night and this morning, but she didn't answer.' She didn't add about the full bath, or that she had rung Lorraine's phone at least seven times since half past eight last night.

'OK, then. I'll be home shortly. Bye.'

Luke put the phone down. Where the hell? he thought. He rang Lorraine's mother, only to be told that both she and Peggy had rung this morning and got no answer. Reassuring Mavis that Lorraine's phone must be broken, he rang Houghton police station, and asked to be put through to Sanderson. Something wasn't right. He could feel it.

CHAPTER SEVENTY-NINE

Stevie had heard about Martin. Secretly he was relieved, and a little pleased, that he was alive, although he'd never let on to Dev, and instead had made some really scathing remarks about him. Dev was also pleased that the kid was alive, but these facts he'd kept to himself.

Most of the night they had been up, walking past the Lumsdons' house over and over. Each time they passed, Dev had punched his left palm with his right fist.

And now they sat on a seat in the park, watching the council workmen mend the broken swings, agreeing with an old woman who had a toddler with her that whoever had done the damage should be hung, drawn and quartered.

Dev sniggered when she walked away and, looking at Stevie, said, 'Bit fucking harsh that, like, hung drawn and quartered. Stupid old cow.'

Stevie shrugged. 'So, er ... what you gonna do now?' he asked, praying that Dev's answer would be that he was moving on.

'Change of plan mate. Think I'll just hang around for a while. Besides, working for that evil cow in the Blue Lion could be very profitable, don't you think?'

Stevie's heart sank. He'd thought that Dev had brought enough havoc to the Lumsdons, and now he'd be gone out of his hair for good. Then he could at least try to sort his life out.

'Why? I thought you were all sorted. Got your revenge, on that copper as well didn't you?'

'Sort of, that's him done, although that kid of his... Now I can imagine some fun with her – but the rest of them ... it just wasn't sweet enough. No, I want the bitch to really pay. This? Well, this is only the fucking beginning.'

Stevie stared in front of him, seeing the girl at Houghton Cut. It was his fault the girl was dead. If only he hadn't shouted, 'There's Claire Lumsdon!' If that motorbike hadn't suddenly come from nowhere at the same time, startling Dev, then perhaps the girl would still be alive. At least, that's what

I'd thought at first, that it was an accident. He turned his head and looked at Dev. But now I'm not so sure.

CHAPTER EIGHTY

Lorraine's throat was sore from reciting poetry most of the night into his tape recorder, but she carried on, knowing that her only hope was to antagonise him enough to bring him in close to her so that she had a fighting chance. He was standing with his back to her, fully clothed. And thank God, she thought, what she had feared hadn't happened. Not yet anyhow, seeing as she was still naked. She cleared her throat and went on, adding her own slant to the poetry.

'The lilies in the field fucking remind me of you.

How blue, how fucking blue are you.

How true, you bastard you.

Now fuck off 'cause I've had enough of you.'

He turned and stared at her. Lorraine stared right back into his eyes.

CHAPTER EIGHTY-ONE

Discharged from the hospital, and promising to rest for a day or two, Luke got to the station as quickly as he could. Reaching the office, he found DI Alison Fyfe talking to Sanderson and Dinwall. She nodded to him as Sanderson and Dinwall both stood up to greet him.

'Good to see you looking so well, DS Daniels. I'll leave it to Sanderson to tell you the latest. Oh, and when DI Hunt comes in, could you please tell her that I would like to see her as soon as possible. Thank you.'

Luke replied with a gruff, 'Yes,' and she turned and left them.

'That bloody woman gets right on my tits,' Dinwall said. Both Sanderson and Luke looked down at his chest. 'Just an expression... Anyhow, glad to see you looking good.'

'Yes, me too.' Sanderson shook Luke's hand. 'Great to have you back.' He glanced at Dinwall, before saying, 'Isn't the boss with you?'

'No. Have either of you heard from her?' They both shook their heads.

'Tried phoning a few times, but there's no

answer, not even voice mail,' Sanderson said. 'We thought she might be at the hospital with you.'

'Not since last night.' Trying not to show just how worried he was, he said, 'So, what did Fyfe have to say?'

'There's no DNA in the car, apart from yours, and it may not have been actually a planned murder, as... Is there something wrong with your gears, Luke?' Dinwall asked.

'No. They're a bit close together. All right when you get used to them. Why?'

Dinwall put his head down, obviously not wanting to answer. Luke looked at Sanderson.

Reluctantly Sanderson said. 'Em, it seems that the new PC sort of er...'

'What.' Luke demanded as Sanderson hesitated.

'Well... He reversed into the wall in the compound. He says it was stuck in reverse.'

'So it might not be murder after all, and the car thief panicked and ran.' Dinwall put in.

Luke sighed. No girl friend... No car... Starting out to be a good day. Looking at Dinwall he went on. 'I think I'll just pop home for a bit, see if Lorraine's turned up there yet.'

'I'll come with you. Hold the fort, Dinwall.' Sanderson shrugged his jacket on and straightened his tie. He had not let on to Dinwall just how worried he was. Lorraine was not the sort of person to just take off. Weird how her phone acted up yesterday morning as well – but that was explained by it not being recharged. That can hardly be today's explanation. He followed Luke out to his car.

'Wrong side, Luke.' By habit, Luke had gone to the driver's side.

'Yeah.' Luke walked round to the other side.

Sanderson told his worries on the way there to a silent Luke, who sat staring out of the windscreen. When they reached the house, he jumped out of the car before it stopped and ran up the path, leaving the door open for Sanderson behind him.

Selina pushed Mickey away and jumped up, straightening her clothes. 'Hi, Dad,' she said, blushing.

'Hi yourself.' He frowned at Mickey, who quickly looked away.

'You all right now, Dad?'

'Yes, I'm fine.'

Selina moved towards him and opened her arms. 'I'm pleased. Don't know what I'd do without you now. I nearly died when Lorraine phoned. So how come you look so good?'

'Still coughing now and then, but it was mostly the drugs some bas ... person spiked me with.' He gave her a cuddle, then holding her at arms' length, said, 'When did you last see Lorraine?'

'Not since before we went away, Dad. She wasn't here when we got back last night. The bath was still full, though, so I guessed she'd been called out in a hurry.'

'Any sign of a disturbance?' Sanderson asked from the doorway. 'Are all of her clothes still here?'

Luke looked at Sanderson. 'I'll check, but she just moved in the day before, so...' He shrugged, then went quickly upstairs, taking them two at a time.

He opened the wardrobe door. It all looked normal to him. She had opted for the right hand side, and his stuff had been relegated to the left. He looked in the drawers. Everything that he knew of was there – her make-up, hairdryer.

He turned to Sanderson. 'Nothing's missing.'

'OK.' Sanderson went downstairs. In the hallway, he took his phone out and dialled the station. Within minutes, her description had been circulated.

CHAPTER EIGHTY-TWO

Vanessa and the older kids had got home at four o'clock in the morning, pleased that the doctors had said that Darren would hopefully make a full recovery. Darren himself had not been able to tell them anything. In fact, it had set them all off crying when he had opened his eyes and didn't know any of them.

Now the house was full of well-wishers. Vanessa escaped into the kitchen for a moment. Leaning with her back against the sink, she breathed deeply. Never had the longing been as great as it had in the early hours of this morning. Unable to stand it any more, she had left the house and walked down to Burnmoor garage. The small bottle of vodka was still unopened, hidden away at the back of the cupboard. In the end, when she had got back home she had resisted the urge and gone to bed, most probably because she was exhausted.

But it was calling to her now.

Her back against the sink she took a deep breath. She would resist. She would. No matter how strong the call.

Everything was fine. Darren was safe, the

docs had said so, even if he had no recollection of what happened and how he came to be in the haunted house in the first place, it made no difference he was going to be alright.

They were all going to be alright.

They had come though time and time again, as a family they were close and strong.

Squaring her shoulders she went back into the sitting room, to be with her family and friends.

CHAPTER EIGHTY-THREE

He stood less than a yard away from her, but Lorraine needed him closer. She looked defiantly up at him, his face red with anger as he glared down at her.

'How dare you!'

'What?' she asked innocently.

'You know what. You've spoilt everything.'

'Don't know what the fucking hell you're talking about.'

His move, when he made it, was sudden. In less than a second, he was towering over her, his face twisted with rage. It was then she took the only chance she could ever see happening.

Quickly, she shot her right foot out and

rammed her heel into the side of his knee. He stared at her in shock. Jumping up, she spun round and, with all the strength she could muster, smashed the side of the chair into him.

The chair broke into bits. He went down, but was far from out. Lorraine herself was in pain where her ribs had bounced off the chair but, ignoring the pain, she kicked him in his stomach (although she had aimed lower) and, using her heel again, caught him behind his ear, knocking him out.

For a moment she could barely breathe. Then, grabbing his knife, she tried to cut the rope binding her arms. This did not prove to be easy. Terrified in case he woke up, she quickly looked around for something else, just as a few fibres of the rope gave way and slackened the dead hold they had on her wrists.

With her shackles off, and her assailant coming round, she grabbed a blanket and wrapped it round herself.

Then she picked up another chair and flung it through the window, screaming for help.

CHAPTER EIGHTY-FOUR

'So it was the brother after all,' Clark said, sitting opposite Lorraine in Luke's house.

She had insisted on being taken home when three squad cars had arrived together. The man had been handcuffed and dragged away, screaming his revenge at Lorraine. It was Carter who shut him up, using his elbow to dig him in the ribs that Lorraine had broken. She now sat content with Luke's arm around her, her mother and Peggy had just left, after Peggy, tears flowing down her face and milking it for all it was worth actually grabbed Sanderson and kissed him.

Clark rose. 'Well done, Lorraine. As ever, above and beyond.' Taking hold of her hand, he shook it. 'I'll see myself out. And I do not want to see either of you at work until next week at the earliest. That is an order.'

Just before the door closed behind him, Sanderson said loudly. 'You need a medal for what you've done, Lorraine.'

'Aye,' Dinwall said, from the opposite corner. 'I'll drink to that. Is there any...? And didn't I say it was him all along.'

'Yes Dinwall so you did.' Lorraine nodded at him. 'But the swine babbled all night long. How proud he was of the fact that since being a kid he had torn the wings off every flying creature he could catch and stitched them onto different species. Cat's heads onto dogs.' She shuddered. 'I don't envy Galashiels police going into that bedroom of his.'

'It was the distance of most of the murders that put me off.' Sanderson said, 'A farm worker you wouldn't suspect.'

'We should have realised that he delivered Farm Foods to a whole lot of shops up and down the country.' Lorraine said. 'Tell you what guys I'll never look at a blue van the same way again. God only knows what he's had in the back of there, the creep.'

For a short time everyone fell silent, Lorraine looked out the window, relishing the fact that she was alive to see the view, but knowing it would be a long time before she would forget the moment he took his clothes off.

She could only think the reason he put them back on, after strutting around the room like a peacock was that he was wary of getting to close to her, a fact that had been his downfall in the end.

Luke squeezed her shoulder. 'It's over now love.'

'Just a minute.' Luke stood up. 'Come with

294

me, Carter.'

A few minutes later, they were all raising their glasses to a tearful Lorraine.

CHRISTMAS EVE

The excitement was building in the Lumsdon household, and Vanessa was every bit as giddy as her children. She had so much planned for tomorrow, nothing could go wrong to spoil it, all that was left to do was pick the turkey up from the butchers, and that task would be complete within the hour. She took the mince pies out of the oven, the smell was delicious, after she'd put them on a tray to cool she hugged herself, everything was going to be wonderful from now on, but best of all Darren was safe and due home later, and better still he was going to be just fine. Although he still could not remember how he came to be in the haunted house.

'Oh God I am so lucky.' She muttered.

'Talking to yourself again mam?' Kerry asked coming into the kitchen and putting her coffee cup into the sink. Turning she leaned against the sink and folded her arms.

'Kerry I just can't believe everything is alright.'

'Well it is, so get used to it.' She grinned at

her mother.

Vanessa heaved a sigh of contentment as she grinned back.

Outside of the Metro centre Jacko and his mates were doing fine, Adam was on his way back with fresh tins for the third time. Jacko had to keep looking away from Len, never before had he seen such a grin on his face, and it kept on getting wider.

'I give it till three o clock, then his face will just disappear down his throat.' Danny whispered.

Jacko nearly choked trying to keep his laugh in at the picture of Len being swallowed by his own throat.

Arriving back Adam handed them all a fresh collecting tin, his grin nearly as wide as Len's.

'You sure you locked the van door?' Danny asked.

'Why aye man, do you think I'm daft or what, not gonna risk all that hard earned dosh getting nicked.'

'Just checking.'

'How much do you reckon we've made?' Len asked. Barely able to stop himself from laughing out loud.

'Wouldn't like to say.' Danny said.

'Why not?'

'In case you're fucking face falls off.'

For the rest of the afternoon, customers to

the Metro centre were met by four of the happiest men wearing Santa outfits on that day.

A few hours later they arrived back at the Seahills. Jacko was the last one to be dropped off, as most of their takings had been in coins, Jacko had two reinforced carrier bags full one in each hand, he set off down his path. Reaching the door he looked to the left, for a moment he frowned. Is that the shit bag standing staring into Vanessa's house? he thought.

He heard laughing, the sound of young girls, then he saw Melanie and Emma skipping up the street. As he watched Melanie spotted Dev and froze.

Jacko felt the hackles rise on the back of his neck. Quickly he opened the door and threw the bags into the house.

Dev never saw Jacko coming.

Dev snarled at Melanie, 'What you looking at you fucking little bitch.'

Her eyes glued to Dev's face, Melanie had not seen her father coming either. Shaking with fear, her heart pounding she took a small step backwards.

'Not so cocky now are you, eh ... are you?' he moved towards her, his hands lifting slowly from his sides.

The words had barely left his mouth when he was grabbed from behind and spun round. The fist smashed into his mouth bursting his lips open and loosening two teeth, the next punch caught his right eye, for a moment he went dizzy and his knees buckled.

'What the fuck.' He yelled, in pain as well as anger. Spitting out blood and steadying himself he swung out and caught Jacko on his ear. 'Who the fucking hell are you?'

Jacko shrugged the blow off and grabbed Dev by his throat, pulling his face forward he snarled. 'I'm Melanie's dad, that's who I am... If you so much as look at her again I'll fucking kill you.'

He nutted Dev, who sank to his knees, just as Melanie reached them. Jacko scooped her up hiding Dev's body from her and carried her home.

Emma ran into the house yelling at the top of her voice, when Vanessa calmed her down enough to understand what she was going on about she and Kerry both went to the window and pulled the curtains open.

'There's nobody there.' Kerry said. 'I hope you're not making it up for attention Emma.'

'Honest I'm not, ask Melanie.'

Vanessa sighed. 'OK, we will tomorrow, but now bath, pyjamas on and bed for Santa.'

Emma hugged her mother. 'OK mam.'

They both watched Emma climb the

stairs. 'Unbelievable.' Kerry said.

Vanessa put her arm around Kerry, and with a smile said. 'Tomorrow is going to be a wonderful day.'

This Large Print Book, for people
who cannot read normal print,
is published under the auspices of

THE ULVERSCROFT FOUNDATION